This Armada book belongs to:

_____

EXPLAINED
_____

JACKIE ON PONY ISLAND

JUDITH M. BERRISFORD

First published in the U.K. in 1977 by
Hodder & Stoughton Ltd., Leicester.
This edition was first published in Armada in 1979 by
Fontana Paperbacks,
14 St. James's Place, London SW1A 1PS.

This impression 1981

© 1961 Judith M. Berrisford.

Printed in Great Britain by
Love & Malcomson Ltd.,
Brighton Road, Redhill, Surrey.

CONTENTS

CHAPTER ONE

RUNAWAY PONY

'Come on, Misty! You can do it if you try.'

I took a 'feel' on the reins as I sat down for the flying change. We were cantering figures-of-eight on the sands and I was determined that my grey pony should get the movement right.

Behind me, my cousin Babs was having problems with her skewbald, Patch. Always wilful, her brown-and-white pony was in no mood for dressage that morning.

Mind you, Misty, too, wasn't in the mood for being schooled. Both ponies had the wind in their tails, and my pony's cat-like ears flicked as the seagulls swooped.

7

'I'm not going to let you beat me, Patch,' I heard Babs declare in exasperation as her pony gave a high-spirited buck. 'I know you want to take the tickle out of your feet, but you've got to do two more figures-of-eight before I let you canter along the beach.'

We circled again. Misty carried out the change neatly, giving Patch a lead. Riding close behind us, Babs was able to get Patch to follow suit. We cantered the figure-of-eight again. Then we reined up and made our ponies trot the outline traced by their own hoof-prints.

'Now for a pipe-opener, Misty,' I told my pony.

Touching her with my heels I set off along the beach. Patch, never wanting to be left behind, pounded alongside. Both ponies were eager to break into gallops, but Babs and I felt that we must exert our wills over their obstinacy for the sake of pony-discipline.

This summer holidays we had decided to practise dressage. So, instead of letting our ponies have their heads, we let them do ten beats full-out. Then we alternated with ten at a controlled, collected canter.

'Look out, Jackie!' Babs suddenly warned. 'Patch is overtaking.'

Next moment she shot past, her pony tossing his head and fighting the bit.

'Sorry,' Babs called over her shoulder. 'I couldn't hold him.'

As Patch passed us, Misty threw up her head,

and, neck extended, broke into a determined gallop. She wasn't going to be beaten by Patch. Not she! She thought that racing along the beach was wonderful.

Showers of wet sand flew from our ponies' drumming hooves while the ringed plovers flew up in clouds before us, and the wind turned the waves into white horses with mane of blown spume.

Misty was gaining on Patch, so the skewbald, hearing her hoof-beats behind him, put on an extra burst of speed. How lucky we were to have such grand ponies, I thought as, neck-and-neck, they thudded towards the rocky point!

'Pony Island here we come!' Babs exclaimed, reining Patch to a trot. 'It's always a thrill to see the Shadow Pony when we round the point.'

'Yes, wonderful!'

We gazed at the grassy slopes of the island. On its rocky headland the lantern glass of the lighthouse winked in the sunlight. The walls of the coastguard cottages showed white against the blue sky.

Anchored boats bobbed in the cove, and, on the hill, behind the castle ruins, a butterfly-kite was fluttering.

'Look!' Babs pointed excitedly. 'There's the Shadow Pony.'

I followed my cousin's gaze to see the shadow which the sun, behind an outcrop of rocks, had cast on the green turf. It was strange. The rocks that caused the shadow did not look like a pony,

9

but when the sun's rays caught them, at a certain angle, they threw the perfect shadow of a galloping pony on the turf.

As we looked, the Shadow Pony seemed so real that we could almost hear its hoof-beats. Then a white cloud momentarily covered the sun and the illusion vanished.

'We were lucky to see it,' I said. 'Another minute and we'd have missed it.'

'If only I'd brought my camera,' said Babs. 'What a shot it would have made with you and Misty in the foreground!'

She broke off to listen. The Shadow Pony had gone but—strange!—we still fancied that we could hear hoof-beats. We looked along the beach. Yes, the hoof-beats were real. Coming towards us was a runaway black Shetland pony, riderless and bridleless, but saddled and with stirrups flying. Obvious his rider had taken a fall, and the Sheltie had bolted.

'Hullo!' I exclaimed. 'Someone's in pony trouble.'

CHAPTER TWO

A BOY IN DISTRESS

I rode to turn the Shetland pony and Babs galloped Patch in an outflanking sweep. Seeing Misty solidly barring his path, the bolting pony swerved to the right. He turned again when he saw Babs and Patch moving to cut him off in that direction. Whinnying, he made for the sandhills.

'Head him into the gully, Jackie,' Babs called, riding in from the left. 'We need to use pincer-tactics now.'

The Sheltie paused. Then he tried to match our strategy with his own cunning. He wasn't going to let himself be cornered, after all. He wheeled and galloped back on his tracks.

Misty and Patch almost collided as Babs and I hastened to head off his retreat. The Sheltie saw us and paused, wondering which way to swerve.

While he hesitated, Babs jumped off Patch and, running, hurled herself at the Sheltie's head. She grabbed his mane, hanging on as he swung away.

'No you don't, my lad.'

My cousin dug her toes into the sand to hold him while I slid down from Misty and ran to help.

11

'Got you!'

I slipped the strap of my haversack round his neck. Then Babs ran to Patch, took off the rope-halter that he was wearing under his bridle and tightened it to fit the Sheltie's head. While I talked soothingly to the pony and fed him a piece of bread from my pocket, Babs put the head-rope over his ears.

'Hey, what about this?' she said. 'He's worked his saddle half-way up his neck.'

Keeping my grip on the Sheltie's halter, I patted him as Babs edged his saddle back into position. I ran the irons up their leathers and pulled up his girth. She was struggling with the buckle as some words, printed with a felt-pen on the leather underside of the saddle-flap, caught my eye: THIS SADDLE BELONGS TO DOUGAL—PONY OF ROBIN LEE. I read the words aloud and the Sheltie's ears flicked.

'You know your name, don't you, Dougal?'

I stroked his nose and we repeated the word 'Dougal' over and over again so that the pony would know he was among friends, despite our firm handling of him.

'Now to restore him to his owner,' said Babs, 'wherever he may be. Come on, Jackie. We'll start by following Dougal's tracks.'

Leading the three ponies, we followed the Shetland's hoof-prints in reverse over the sands, past the breakwaters and round the tide-pools. We lost the trail over some shingle but picked it up again in the soft sand by the flattened marram grass at the edge of the sandhills. We followed the hoof-prints through a forestry plantation of young firs, stumbling here and there over the ruts.

'Robin . . . Robin Lee!' I called. 'Are you there? We've got your pony. Shout back if you can hear us.'

We called half-a-dozen times before we heard a voice answer. 'I'm over here. Follow the stream. I've hurt my ankle and I can't walk. You'll have to help me!'

We made our way across the tussocky grass to the stream. On the bank, a boy was sitting, holding a ponyless bridle. He looked about nine years old, a forlorn jeans-clad figure with freckled face under a mop of curly fair hair.

'Thanks a lot for catching Dougal,' the boy said gratefully. 'If you can help me on his back, I can ride home, I think.'

Gamely he struggled to rise.

'Not so fast, my lad,' Babs cautioned as, moistening her handkerchief in the stream, she dabbed some blood from his forehead. 'Let's see how badly you're hurt.'

'You've got a nasty cut,' I said. 'What happened?'

'Dougal threw me,' the boy explained. 'Then I was trying to catch him when I caught my foot in a rabbit hole and cut my head on a stone.'

'But how did Dougal lose his bridle?' Babs asked, mystified.

'He doesn't like getting his feet wet,' the boy said. He winced as Babs cleaned the cut, and then rinsed out the handkerchief in the stream and put in round his swollen ankle to act as a cold compress. 'I suppose I was asking for it, in a way, trying to ride him through the stream.'

'And he jibbed, I suppose,' prompted Babs.

'He went berserk,' groaned the boy. 'He kicked up his heels, pitched me forward and I sailed over his head taking the reins with me. Then he managed to wriggle out of his bridle, broke free and bolted.'

'Goodness!' I exclaimed. 'Has he ever done that before?'

'Well, yes; it's a habit of his,' the boy sighed. 'It doesn't matter so much while he's my pony, but, you see, he's probably got to be sold and nobody will want to buy him if I don't succeed in schooling him out of his worst habits.'

'You've got a problem,' I said, noticing the

wayward glint in Dougal's eye. 'I wish you luck. You'll need it.'

I knew Shetland ponies had a reputation for being obstinate. They weren't always ideal mounts for young children, I thought. Between us, Babs and I hoisted the boy off the ground, so that he could get his leg over the saddle.

'We'll lead Dougal for you and see you safely home,' said Babs.

'Is it far?' I asked.

'Only about a mile,' the boy said, picking up Dougal's reins. 'My brother and sister and I are staying on Pony Island.' He winced as he tried to put his injured foot into the stirrup. Suddenly he looked troubled. 'My brother Dave's going to be upset when he realises I'm out of action with this sprained ankle,' he told us. 'You see, while we've been staying at Seashell Cottage we've been using our ponies to give rides on the beach. We're trying to make the money for their winter keep. Now, I shan't be able to lead the customers up and down for some time.'

'I suppose not,' I agreed. 'What bad luck!'

'It's more than bad luck,' groaned Robin. 'It's a disaster. Dave will be wild.'

'It wasn't your fault that Dougal threw you,' I consoled.

'Well, it was, in a way,' Robin confessed. 'Dave and Felicity wanted me to go down on the beach with them this afternoon to take the money for the rides while Dougal was tied up behind the cottage. You see, he's not reliable, and Dave

15

doesn't think we ought to let other people ride him unless he or Felicity are able to supervise. They were so busy giving rides on their own ponies that we couldn't have used Dougal.'

'So you thought you'd go off on your own and give him some schooling to make him more reliable?' I prompted.

'That's it,' said Robin. 'I told Dave and Felicity that I wanted to stay in this afternoon to finish the model of a ship I'm making for Dad. It's his birthday next month. He was in the Navy, you see, and I bought a model-making kit of Dad's frigate. I thought he'd like to have it in his room. I worked on the model for a couple of minutes. Then I did what I secretly intended to do all the time—went out to school Dougal.'

'And now comes the moment of reckoning, I suppose,' I sympathised, pushing Misty away as she tried to nuzzle my pocket.

'You're right there,' Robin agreed. 'Dave's apt to get rather cross these days. I suppose I can't blame him. He's got a lot on his mind. Mum and Dad had to take a living-in job at a golf club. So Dave's in charge of Felicity, me and the ponies and you know how it is—trouble and ponies go together.'

'Don't we know!'

Then Babs and I exchanged glances. We'd both had the same brainwave. How wonderful it would be if we could persuade Dave to let us help with their beach-pony enterprise!

CHAPTER THREE

DAVE HAS HIS DOUBTS

'There! How's that?'

I put a wooden box under Robin's foot as, half an hour later, he sat in a folding chair outside the door of Seashell Cottage. We had tied up our ponies and Babs had dabbed iodine, from a first-aid kit, on his cut, and bandaged his forehead.

'Just the job,' Robin said as he gingerly touched the bandage. 'But I do feel a chump, sitting here, doing nothing useful. Dave and Felicity are going to get such a shock when they come up the path from the beach and see me like this. Golly, here they are!'

Dave, who was about sixteen, and an older edition of Robin, was astride a black gelding as he came in sight along the sandy path. Behind him, auburn-haired Felicity rode a slim-legged bay.

In her hand was a pole to which had been fixed a piece of painted plywood, bearing the bold lettering: PONY RIDES.

'Goodness!' Dave groaned, when he saw Robin. 'More trouble. Whatever have you done to yourself?'

'Don't be alarmed,' Babs said quickly. 'Robin may be bandaged, but he isn't seriously hurt, just a cut forehead and a sprained ankle. We sort of rescued him.'

'Did you indeed?' said Dave. 'So instead of model-making, Robin took Dougal out on his own! That's typical.' He looked quizzically at Babs and me. 'And where do you two girls fit into the picture?'

'We caught Dougal when he bolted and then brought Robin back here,' I explained.

'Trust Robin and Dougal to cause the maximum amount of trouble!' Dave shook his head in disapproval. 'It's always happening.'

'We didn't mind,' Babs broke in. 'In fact we were only too glad to help.'

While Babs was speaking, Dave's black pony shifted his feet restlessly. Dave said: 'Don't be impatient, Havoc,' and took off his saddle and bridle.

Meanwhile Felicity, who had already unsaddled her pony, smiled at Babs and me in a friendly way.

'You seem to have done jolly well,' she said warmly as though to make up for her brother's shortness of manner. She opened the cottage door. 'Why not come in and have some lemonade?'

'I do think you are lucky.' Babs sighed, as she gazed around the pink-washed sitting-room with the cheerful rugs on the stone floor, blue and

18

white pottery gleaming on the dresser, and the comfortable chintzy armchairs. 'I envy you.'

'This must be a super place to stay,' I said. 'What a wonderful time you must have, giving pony rides on Pony Island beach.'

'Yes, I suppose things could be worse.' Felicity sounded doubtful as she sipped her lemonade. 'Actually though, we're going through a bad patch.'

'How's that?' I asked.

'We've had a family disaster.' Felicity's hazel eyes looked troubled. 'The sort of thing you read about in the newspapers but never imagine's going to happen to you.'

'Our home was burnt down,' put in Robin. 'Everything went up in flames, the furniture, our books, most of our clothes. The lot!'

'Oh, for heaven's sake, you two!' Dave's voice cut across our murmurs of sympathy as he came into the cottage. 'These two girls don't want to hear about our family troubles.'

'But we do,' Babs assured him. 'It sounds dreadful. I can imagine how we'd feel if it had happened to us.'

'I dare say, but it hasn't.' Dave ran an impatient hand through his wavy chestnut hair. 'And it doesn't help if Felicity goes on moaning and everybody sympathises. We've got to put it behind us and make a go of things.'

'Dave's right,' agreed Robin, glaring at his sister. 'Why do you have to remind us by moaning all the time?'

Felicity threw a cushion at her younger brother. 'You're always on my side until Dave says his piece. Then you agree with him, and it's two to one. That's what comes of being the only girl in the family.'

'That's right, bicker in front of strangers!' Dave seemed almost at the end of his tether. 'Show the world that the Lee family can't cope with troubles.'

'If you'd tell us all about it, we might be able to help you,' Babs said undaunted.

'You *have* helped us.' Dave walked to the door and opened it. 'You caught Dougal and rescued Robin. That's your good turn for the day. Now, if you don't mind, perhaps you'll leave us to sort out our own problems in our own way.'

'Is that how you really want it to be?' I asked in dismay. 'Won't you give us a chance to help?' I glanced over Dave's shoulder to Robin and Felicity who were now looking woebegone. 'Why can't we be friends?'

'We *are* friends,' Dave said in exasperation. 'But right now we've got enough to cope with.'

Then he broke off, and Babs and I held our breath as Dave looked keenly at us. We knew what he was trying to decide. Would we be the kind of pony-girls who would be a help—or a nuisance?'

'Mind you, if you do help, you've got to get your Mum's and Dad's permission,' Dave said at last. 'And, to be quite honest, I'd better explain that it isn't so much you two girls that we need. It's your ponies. Now this is our idea . . .'

Dave went on to explain that he and his brother and sister needed to make some money during the summer holidays. They were in desperate straits because their house had been underinsured when it was burnt down. Their mother and father had managed to get living-in jobs as steward and stewardess at a golf club but a condition of the job was that no children were allowed. So, for the time being, their father, who had recently come out of the Navy, had rented a holiday cottage for them on Pony Island. Luckily there was grass on the island for the ponies to graze. So, for the summer at least, they were still able to keep the ponies.

'Unless we can make two hundred pounds or so, we shan't have enough money for their winter keep,' Dave went on. 'Then we'd have to get rid of them. Lots of pony owners are in the same fix, with pony-nuts and hay scarce and expensive. So it might be impossible to find anyone to buy our ponies—except horsemeat dealers.'

We felt stunned. This was the worst thing that could happen to any pony owner.

'We'll do anything to help,' I said, at last.

'Anything,' added Babs.

'Yes, that's what I thought you'd say,' Dave said. 'But I'll be quite frank. I've had pony-girls before and they've all been flops. You may prove to be more trouble than you're worth. You may

21

even be a couple of teenage catastrophes. I know I'm taking a risk.'

We refused to be dampened by Dave's doubts. So we listened intently as he told us that quite a number of children visited Pony Island by the ferry-boat each day. The pony rides were popular and the demand couldn't be satisfied with only three ponies.

'So we'd like to borrow your ponies, and you as well,' he said. 'Now, because it's possible to ride across the causeway only at certain states of the tide, you'd have to stay on Pony Island with us at Seashell Cottage. You and Babs and Felicity would shake-down in the cottage, and Robin and I would use the tent. You'd have to be prepared to act sensibly and work hard. Well, what do you say? Are you game to have a go?'

CHAPTER FOUR

BEACH PONIES

'Whoa, Misty! Not so fast.'

I tried to hold my pony's lead rope with one hand and, with the other, to help a young mother lift her three-year-old girl into the saddle.

Misty snorted. She was raring to go.

Havoc, Moonlight and Patch were already half-way along the beach with riders, so my pony didn't want to be left behind. She circled impatiently while I was trying to adjust the leathers.

The snag was that there were not enough holes to make the stirrup short enough. The little girl's feet would not even reach the loops. So, warning the mother to hold tightly to her child, and, keeping a short grip on the lead rope, I led my pony along the sands.

'That's right, dear,' the mother was encouraging her daughter. 'You're having a lovely ride.' She turned to me. 'It's a good idea having pony rides on the island. Will you be here every day?'

'I hope so,' I replied, crossing my fingers for luck as I remembered how difficult it had been to persuade Mummy and Daddy to let us stay at Seashell Cottage.

Finally, they'd half-agreed. 'Well, suppose you try it for a few days,' Daddy had said, 'and see how you go on.'

So that morning, Babs and I had ridden over, loading our saddle-bags with spare clothes and provisions, and carrying bulging haversacks on our backs. We'd been in good time for the low-tide crossing of the causeway, and here we were on the job, helping the Lees with their pony-ride venture. There was all the afternoon ahead of us, and more holiday-makers and their children were arriving by ferry every hour.

Pony-business was brisk on Pony Island. So far so good.

As I turned Misty by the rock pool, at the far end of the curving bay, I could see Babs, Felicity and Dave, leading their ponies towards me with more delighted children astride.

Already a queue of would-be riders was forming by a card table which bore a sign that read: BOOK YOUR PONY RIDES HERE.

From a folding chair, Robin, a sticking plaster on his forehead, was handing out tickets in exchange for ten-pence pieces which he was adding to the growing pile in an old toffee tin.

Behind him, Dougal, reins fastened to the canvas back of the chair, was standing looking puzzled, wondering why he and Robin weren't joining in the fun.

'Why can't I ride this pony?' I heard one small boy ask, patting Dougal, as I returned Misty to base. 'I don't want to ride any of the others. This

24

one's the right size for me, and he's taken a liking
to me. Look!'

He chuckled as Dougal nuzzled against his
shoulder.

'Hey, stop it,' the boy laughed. 'Your whiskers
are tickling me.'

At that moment, a ten-year-old girl assured me that she was a good rider, and that she could manage Misty on her own. So I handed over my pony to her and suggested to Robin that I gave Dougal's new pal a ride on the Sheltie.

As I helped the boy into the saddle, he told me that his name was Kenny. I adjusted the stirrups, showed him how to hold Dougal's reins, and grasped the lead-rope near his head.

'All set, Kenny?' I asked, and the boy nodded happily as we set off.

Dougal stepped out jauntily. His ears were neatly pricked and he was intent on quickening his pace. No doubt he was eager to catch up with Misty who, with the ten-year-old girl aloft, was now three-quarters of the way to the rock pool.

Havoc, Patch and Moonlight had already got to the turning-point and, as they started back, Dougal threw up his head and gave a whinny of greeting. Havoc whickered and I saw Dave hang on to his head to slow him as he tried to quicken his pace.

Then Dougal began to pull strongly and I had to put all my weight on the lead-rope to hold him back.

'Can't we go a bit faster?' Kenny urged. 'Make him run?'

That was the last thing that I wanted Dougal to do. I let go of the lead-rope and grasped the Shetland's rein near the bit. Suddenly the Shetland gave a twist of his head. He seemed to spit out the bit and wriggle his head-band over his ears in the same moment. Then the cheek-piece went slack and the nose-band dropped downwards. A second later, I found myself holding an empty bridle while Dougal was dragging the lead-rope through the fingers of my other hand as he took off in a canter.

'Hang on to the saddle, Kenny,' I urged. 'Don't let go.'

Dougal was now well away, cantering determinedly in the direction of his friend, Havoc.

Kenny gamely clung on and I was thankful that I'd had the patience to shorten the stirrup-leathers so that his sandalled feet fitted into the irons.

Meanwhile, having seen what was happening, Dave broke into a run, causing Havoc to trot while his plump girl-rider quivered like a jelly on his back.

As soon as Dougal came within nose-touching distance of Havoc, the Sheltie slackened his pace. Both ponies halted and seemed to confer while their riders exchanged relieved grins and I put on Dougal's bridle once more.

'Again, again!' piped Kenny, who had decided that he had thoroughly enjoyed the excitement. 'Smashing! Can't we do it again?'

'Not if I have anything to do with it,' Dave said, with breathless exasperation. 'And listen, young fellow,' he spoke sternly to Kenny who grinned back, unabashed, 'next time you have a ride, you'll come to me and not to the girls. Then

I'll decide which pony you can have and I'll keep an eye on you too, my lad.'

I almost quailed as Dave looked from Kenny to me in reproof. 'For Pete's sake, Jackie, try to be responsible. The reason we don't often use Dougal for rides is because he's only a hundred per cent reliable when he's got me to control him. So don't go acting on your own initiative. Understand?'

'Yes, Dave,' I said meekly. 'Anything you say. You're the boss.'

Several hours later the last ferry-load of holiday-makers left the island. The few families who were renting the other holiday cottages were indoors eating their supper. The ponies had been unsaddled and turned loose on the island to graze. Now Babs and I were helping Felicity to prepare a meal of baked beans, sausages and toast.

Meanwhile Dave was putting up a ridge-tent while Robin hopped round hammering in tent pegs. The boys were camping out, leaving their bedroom in the cottage free for Babs and me. They had chosen a sheltered site for their tent, ten metres from the cottage on a level grassy ledge, half-way up the rising ground.

'Supper's ready, boys,' Babs called, putting the laden plates on to the table while I poured cocoa into the mugs, and Felicity produced a bowl of apples.

It was an enjoyable meal, with lots of light-hearted chatter. Even Dave seemed relaxed and to have decided that, on balance, Babs and I had made a fair contribution to the success of the day.

'Leave the washing up till later,' he directed as we cleared the table. 'I want to find out how much money we've made today.'

He tipped out the contents of the toffee tin and we counted the money into piles.

'Four pounds sixty, if we count that Irish ten pence piece,' said Felicity. 'That's more than twice as much as we took yesterday.'

'Yippee!' whooped Robin. 'Being able to use Misty and Patch as well makes all the difference.'

Dave scooped the money into a plastic bag and Felicity tied it round with a scarlet hair-ribbon.

'Now to find a good hiding place for the loot,' Dave said, pleased with the day's work, and I was happy because, for the first time, I was seeing him in a hopeful and contented mood.

'I do want everything to turn out well for the Lees,' Babs said as we snuggled down in our bedroom under the eaves of Seashell Cottage that night.

'Me too,' I agreed. 'They've had such bad luck. It must be terrible to be separated from their parents and have no real home.'

Just then the beam from the lighthouse lit up the ceiling as the lantern swept round on its revolving base. I raised myself on one elbow to look out of the open window, and I saw the shaft fall across the green canvas of the tent.

I heard the murmur of the boys' voices, Robin's light, but drowsy with sleep, and Dave's more grown-up, but still youthfully eager and full of plans.

Beyond the tent, under the lea of the hill, the ponies were huddled. I could make out Misty and Patch standing nose-to-tail with Moonlight beside them. Felicity's bay seemed to have made friends with Patch and Misty as ponies of similar size and temperament often do.

A little way off, stood the larger, darker shape of Havoc, with, beside him, the small, sturdy outline of Dougal.

'Sleep well, ponies,' I murmured, settling down again in my bed. 'You've got a busy day to-morrow. A lot depends on you.'

CHAPTER FIVE

JINXED AGAIN

'Give me your foot, Misty.'

I ran my hand gently down my pony's forearm to grasp her leg above the knee. I pressed with my elbow against her until she shifted her weight to her other leg. Then I picked up her right leg in my left hand, and took hold of her foot, bending it upwards.

I took the hoof-pick from my pocket and ran it round the inside of her hoof, scooping out the sand and dirt, being careful not to touch the frog, the sensitive part of a pony's hoof.

Meanwhile, Babs and Felicity were brushing Moonlight and Patch, and Dave was cleaning out Havoc's feet.

Robin, who could now put his foot to the ground without wincing, hobbled round Dougal, getting together his grooming kit.

Babs and I had already been on the island for four days. Yesterday my parents had come over by ferry to see us. Felicity had shown them over the cottage; and they'd joined us on the beach; Daddy had gone for a swim, and Mummy had a ride on Havoc. Daddy then volunteered to take over Dougal, and his customers, for half-an-hour, while I rode Misty to the ferry-jetty to collect the sack of groceries which had been sent across from the mainland.

Mummy and Daddy had enjoyed themselves so much that they didn't go back until the last ferry.

Later, when we were counting out the takings after supper, Dave looked across at Babs and me.

'We're doing very well, thanks to Misty and Patch,' Dave said, sorting the tenpenny pieces into pound piles. 'I must say that I'm relieved that you two pony-girls haven't turned out to be the blight I'd expected. Of course, it's early days yet, but you do seem to be shaping quite well. Rather different, in fact, from the eager-beaver run of pony-girl helpers who queued up to get in the way when we were living at Broad Green before the house burnt down. So keep up the good work!

Encouraged by Dave's unexpected appreciation, we threw ourselves into the pony-ride venture more keenly than ever.

We had a busy morning. The weather was fine and clear, and the ferries were crowded. The ponies carried a variety of riders in an almost non-stop succession.

Once Misty was given a nasty jab in her mouth with the bit, while Havoc was kicked unduly because his rider was under the misapprehension that he was sluggish. The truth was that the

young rider had him on such a tight rein that
Havoc thought she wanted him to stop.

When we unsaddled the ponies at lunchtime
Babs discovered a slight swelling on Patch's back.

'Look at this,' she called in dismay. 'Patch's
saddle must have been slipping.'

'Or perhaps the swelling could have been
caused by Patch carrying so many riders of different weights,' put in Dave.

He ran his fingers over the skewbald's back to
explore the swelling.

'I should bathe it with salt and water,' he
decided.

'Would seawater do?' I asked.

33

'I don't see why not.' Dave soaked his handkerchief in a tide pool. 'Here! Try this.'

Babs firmly applied the compress, and Patch turned his head with a jerk.

'Yes, that stings a bit,' Babs said as her pony twitched the muscles of his back, 'but the salt will toughen the skin and it'll soon feel easier. I'll bathe it again at teatime.'

Dave shook his head. 'It's no use letting him carry riders until his back is better,' he said firmly. 'He's earned a rest.'

Babs slipped the bit out of Patch's mouth, and tethered him to the LITTER PENALTY sign where he would be in the shade and, no doubt, get the pats and attention of the holiday children to stop him from feeling forsaken.

Two days later Dave decided that Patch was fit to work. To stop the pony's back getting rubbed again, he produced a sheepskin numnah.

'I used this for Havoc before Dad gave me a new saddle,' he explained. 'Why not borrow the sheepskin and put it under Patch's saddle to act as a shock-absorber?'

Several young customers accompanied us down the track and others were waiting for us on the beach. Soon we were busy, leading the ponies up and down while the money in the toffee tin piled up satisfactorily.

'Every tinful is a step nearer ensuring winter keep for Havoc, Moonlight and Dougal,' Babs said, dashing to place another forty pence in Robin's tin. 'It's super to be enjoying ourselves and to feel useful at the same time.'

'Yes,' I agreed, 'and this time our efforts to help don't seem to be jinxed. Perhaps our bad luck was well and truly banished by that Lucky Horseshoe Charm that you gave me last Christmas, Babs.'

Little did I realise that pony-trouble was just around the corner . . .

A few minutes later, two more children wanted rides; and I had to shorten Misty's stirrups for the younger one—a boy of about nine. For the next half-hour I was kept busy and didn't have a chance to talk to Babs because we were at different parts of the beach.

I was half-way to the tide pool, and Babs had just started on her way back when there was a commotion from Havoc, Moonlight and Dougal who were waiting for their next riders.

Havoc snorted, Dougal neighed and Moonlight reared.

'Jackie! Babs!' I heard Dave call frantically. 'Hurry! Come and give us a hand.'

Misty's rider looked startled as I turned her round.

'Don't worry,' I said. 'I've got you safe.'

Then I saw the reason for the ponies' panic. A black dog, excited and out of control, was running among them, barking and snapping. Dave released Havoc's head and made a dive to catch the dog. It dodged out of the way, and darted to nip the gelding's heels whereupon Havoc, with a squeal, cannoned into Moonlight.

Several young children were shouting and screaming and Dougal started to buck. Dave made another dive and tried to catch the frenzied

dog by the collar. He missed and the dog ran at Patch who was just coming back.

Patch shied. His rider lost her stirrups and threw her arms round the skewbald's neck, wailing with fright. Meanwhile Babs did her best to save the child from falling, and at the same time, soothe Patch. Then the dog went for Misty who tucked in her hind-quarters and spun round. Her ears flapped back and she faced the dog, ready to send him off with her teeth if he ran at her again.

'Get off, you horrid dog!' shouted Babs, picking up a handful of sand, and throwing it well to the side of the dog to deter him.

'You wicked girl!' came a harsh voice. 'You might have blinded my dog.'

I spun round to see a plump woman with dyed, straw-like hair and a cutaway sunfrock from which her pink flesh bulged. She was advancing on Babs angrily swinging a dog-lead.

Patch reared, thinking the woman was about to strike him, and the small girl rider slid off over his tail to land with a splash into a tide-pool.

Her screams added to the dog's threatening barks and Babs' and the woman's angry voices. They made such a noise that I couldn't hear myself think. This was a pony-nightmare, and we were in the middle of it.

'It's all your fault,' Babs told the woman. 'We were having a super time until your dog came on the scene. Why don't you train him properly? Or put him on a lead, so that he isn't a danger?'

'A danger!' the woman echoed, red in the face. 'It's the ponies who are the danger—with irresponsible teenagers in charge of them. It's a disgrace!'

Suddenly she looked closely at Babs. 'I've seen

37

you before, somewhere, haven't I? And your blessed pony was a nuisance then.'

I glanced at Babs in puzzlement. My cousin usually told me everything, especially where ponies were concerned. Was the woman mistaken, perhaps?

Just then the dog ran, barking, at Dougal who threw up his head and jibbed. So instead of answering the woman, Babs ran to the Shetland to make sure he did not kick the dog. I had the impression that Babs was relieved not to have to reply to the question.

'Please, please!' I begged. 'Do put your dog on the lead.'

'Why should I?' the woman retorted. 'He's as much right to run about this beach as anyone. Probably more so——' She turned, calling over her shoulder to her dog. 'Come on, Tweetie.' Then she paused and added for our benefit: 'You've no right to have ponies on this beach at all.'

Just then, Dave having handed over Havoc to Felicity, came running up.

'Be quiet, Babs,' he said, as my cousin opened her mouth to retort to the woman. 'You've said more than enough.'

'She certainly has,' declared the woman. 'I've never been spoken to in such a way in the whole of my life. If you're in charge of this unruly rabble, young man, all I can say is you should set a better example to your helpers or teach them better manners.'

'I'm sorry——' Dave began to apologise, but his voice was drowned by a forthright shout from a tough-looking boy who had pushed to the front of the group to stand defiantly in front of the angry woman.

'Why don't you belt up and clear off, you silly old moo—and take your wild woggy with you?'

'I've never been so insulted. Never!' The woman rounded on us. You'll regret this—all of you!'

CHAPTER SIX

ORDERED OFF PONY ISLAND

'I'm sorry, Dave, truly I am,' Babs apologised as we turned the ponies loose that evening. 'You're probably right. That boy wouldn't have been so rude if I hadn't given the woman a piece of my mind.'

'Oh, who cares?' Robin groaned, folding Dougal's girth over the seat of his saddle. 'She's probably miles away by now and we may never see her again.'

'I know,' said Babs, 'but I ought to have been polite whatever the provocation. I did let Dave down. And I suppose the woman did have a point of view. After all, from where she was standing, she might really have thought that I threw sand in the dog's face.'

'Jinxed!' I said. 'That's what we were and no wonder.' I turned to my cousin. 'I've just discovered that I've lost my Lucky Horseshoe charm. It must have fallen out of my pocket during all the pony bother. That's enough to double-jinx us.'

'Treble-jinx us!' Dave broke his moody silence to point to the end cottage of the row. 'Look!'

There, in the upstairs window, spotlighted in

the rays of the setting sun, paws on the window-ledge, was the black dog, his head following our every move.

'Tweetie!' I groaned. 'What bad luck! He and his mistress must be staying here. She must have rented the cottage.'

'Yes—and oh gosh, there she is, too!' Robin gasped.

Our dismay must have shown in our faces as we gaped at the vision of the straw-haired, pink-faced plump woman.

To add to our consternation, she rapped on the pane and gestured. Then, opening the window, she put her head out.

'My son and I are coming round to your cottage in half an hour,' she called. 'We want to have a word with you.'

'Two minutes to blast off,' Robin said nearly half an hour later.

'And here we are,' added Babs, 'all washed, tidied-up and sitting like a lot of stuffed dummies.'

'Just waiting to be told off,' I added. 'And all of us faint with hunger because we can't start cooking our supper until they've been.'

'Stand by for the count-down,' Robin broke in dramatically, his eyes on the second hand of the super watch his father had given him for a homecoming present when he left the sea. 'Five, four, three, two, one, zero, *blast off*!'

We gazed at the window, waiting and dreading

the shadows that would fall across it, but all we saw were the hollyhocks swaying in the breeze.

'They're five minutes late already.' Dave looked defeated as he glanced at his watch. 'This is a real war of nerves.'

We almost jumped out of our skins as there was a loud knock on the front door.

'You answer it.' Felicity nudged a reluctant Dave. 'You're the oldest.'

'Oh, dear, they've brought Tweetie, too,' Babs

whispered as we heard paws scrabbling at the front door, and, next moment, the door swung open.

We looked up at the straw-haired woman and a youth who was holding Tweetie on a lead. He was about nineteen and was trendily dressed in white flared trousers, an immaculate black blazer and a light-blue cravat threaded through a snake-ring. To complete the foppish picture he was wearing, on his left hand, a ring with a stone as big as a jujube. He took off his dark glasses to reveal beady, greedy eyes.

I groaned. Never in my life had I seen anyone who looked less horsy. I knew we couldn't expect much sympathy from him.

The youth and his mother made no attempt to sit down, but seemed to loom over us. His mother looked at each of us coldly in turn. Then her gaze rested on Robin.

'I'm not sure whether or not you're the young boy who was so rude to me on the beach this morning——' she began.

Robin blushed guiltily despite his innocence. 'That wasn't me,' he flustered. 'That was a different boy altogether. He wasn't anything to do with us. We were horrified when he called you a "silly old moo".'

Dave hurriedly tried to retrieve the situation. 'We did try to apologise there and then,' he put in, 'but we were busy trying to keep the ponies under control. It was difficult with your dog upsetting them, you see.'

'Ponies!' she echoed, snatching Tweetie's lead from her son and jerking him to his feet as the dog tried to lie down. 'That's what we want to talk to you about. Our dog doesn't get on with ponies. Doesn't like them. Mind you, I don't object to them in their proper place—which isn't a public beach.'

'Oh, yes, it is,' Babs broke in, a gleam in her eyes. 'Lots of beaches have donkeys or ponies. Seaside holidays wouldn't be the same if children couldn't have rides on the beach. Ask any of the families who come to the island.'

'Shut up, Babs,' said Dave, 'you've done enough harm as it is. I've already told you—'

'Why should Babs shut up?' Felicity interrupted, glaring at her brother. 'She's right. Why don't you tell this woman, Dave? You're outspoken enough with us.'

'I don't want to seem impolite.' Dave stood up and faced the woman. 'But the girls do have a point, you know. You do seem to be rather unreasonable.'

'Unreasonable!' the woman repeated. 'Well, one thing is definite. You can't have ponies on this island.'

'No ponies on Pony Island!' Babs exclaimed. 'Why not? This is just where they ought to be. Besides, who are you to say whether there ought to be any ponies here or not?'

'Who am I?' the woman echoed. She turned to her son. 'You tell them, Cedric.'

'Ma's in charge here,' the youth told us. 'You

44

see my aunty's gone to Australia to see her daughter. Aunty owns everything on the island, these cottages, all the grazing and the beach down to the high-water mark. She asked Ma to keep an eye on Pony Island until she gets back.'

'Then your mother must be Mrs Chivers,' Dave said, aghast. 'Dad had a letter to say she was in temporary charge. Oh, gosh!' he groaned. 'Please sit down, both of you. Can't we talk this over?'

'There's nothing more to say, young man.' The woman looked at Dave sternly. 'When your father wrote to my sister and asked her to let this cottage for the summer, he didn't say anything about ponies. Nor did he mention that a pack of children would be here without any grown-ups to keep them in order.'

'What a shock for us!' added the youth. 'Ma and I arrive today to take over, and what do we find? A tent at the back of the cottage; five children; five ponies; rides on the beach; litter everywhere.'

'We didn't leave the litter,' Dave said quietly. 'We kept cleaning it up.'

'Yes, for our benefit, no doubt,' said Mrs Chivers.

'Oh, why must we argue?' Felicity pleaded. 'Can't we be friends? Please let us stay.'

'Impossible.' Mrs Chivers turned to the door. 'I'm sorry, but you and the ponies will all have to go. The sooner the better. Tomorrow, if possible.'

45

I put an arm round Felicity who was almost in tears.

'What's going to happen to us?' she demanded, her lip quivering. 'We haven't any home. It burned down! The ponies haven't anywhere to go and nor have we.'

'That's your problem,' declared Mrs Chivers. 'Not mine.'

She turned to her son. 'You're taking me out to dinner at the Ferry Inn,' she reminded him. 'We're supposed to be on holiday. We've got to enjoy ourselves. That's what my sister said when she went gallivanting off to Australia. Come on do, Cedric. We can't be wasting any more time on these kids.'

CHAPTER SEVEN

PANIC STATIONS

As soon as the Chivers were out of hearing we just had to give vent to our feelings.

'Silly old——' began Robin.

'Sssh! Don't say it,' broke in Felicity. 'We mustn't even think it. It may be the truth, but, somehow, we've got to try not to hate her, so that we can keep the peace.'

'Why bother?' Babs sighed. 'This time to-morrow all of us and the ponies will be off Pony Island. Banished for ever!'

'What's going to become of us then?' Felicity turned pleadingly to her older brother, who, so far had been silent. 'Don't just sit there, Dave. For goodness' sake say something. What do you think's going to happen?'

'Homeless!' Dave said defeatedly. 'That's what we'll be.' He stared hoplessly at his brother and sister. 'All three of us and the ponies. If only Babs had had the sense to shut up. Then Mrs C. might not have been so difficult.'

I avoided catching Babs' eyes. I knew how she must be feeling. We'd known the Lees for only a short while; yet we'd become so involved in their troubles and liked them so much, that

we just couldn't bear the thought of their pony-
ride venture failing, and—even worse—that they
and the ponies would have nowhere to go. We'd
wanted so much to help. Yet, somehow, it seemed
that, as usual, we'd only managed to make mat-
ters worse.

I gazed bleakly out of the window. A gloomy
cloud seemed to have come over the sun: no
silver lining there, I thought, no Shadow Pony to
lighten our mood.

I turned to my cousin to ask the question that
had been puzzling me ever since our first en-
counter with Mrs. Chivers.

'What's the mystery, Babs?' I asked. 'Have
you ever seen the Chiverses before?'

'Yes, I have.' Babs' eyes lightened with in-
trigue. 'It was at the Marston Post Office two
weeks ago. I was buying a postal order to send
off my subscription to *Horseshoes*. The Chiverses
were there and I distinctly remember her saying
to the dog: "Don't pull so, Tweetie." I remembered because I thought what a soppy name for
a dog.'

'What happened then?' prompted Robin.

'Well, Cedric was wearing a dazzling red
blazer, and I heard him tell the woman behind
the counter that he and his mother had arranged
for letters to be addressed to them at the Marston
Post Office.'

'Big deal,' sighed Robin. 'Is that all?'

'No, of course not,' said Babs. 'This is the
really fishy part of it all. The woman behind the

counter asked their name and Mrs Chivers broke in and said: "Gumby".'

'Gumby,' I echoed, 'are you sure?'

'Absolutely,' declared Babs, 'because Mrs Chivers spelt the name out. They were handed a few letters. Meanwhile another assistant had given me my postal order, so the Chiverses, alias the Gumbys, left the post office at the same time as I did.'

'That's when Patch came into the picture, was it?' I put in.

Babs nodded. 'I'd left him tied to the railings and I suppose he was blocking the pavement—and I know ponies aren't supposed to be on pavements but I'd hoped I needn't be many minutes.'

'Then what?' Robin asked.

'Well Patch moved sideways,' said Babs, 'and I suppose Mrs Chivers thought he was going to tread on Tweetie, so she turned to me and told me off for obstructing the pavement and leaving my pony tied up outside the post office.'

'You never told me about it, Babs,' I pointed out.

'It didn't seem to have any significance then,' Babs replied. 'Besides, I knew I'd done wrong ponywise and you'd think I was an idiot.'

'This has the makings of a super mystery,' piped Robin.

'Rot!' Dave, who had been silent up to now, broke in definitely. 'Next moment you'll be saying that the Chiverses are impostors and that they're up to some villainy. It all happened a couple of weeks ago, in a busy post office, with a lot of other things going on at the same time, and even if Babs didn't mishear the name Gumby, the Chiverses might have been picking up letters for a friend who couldn't get to the post office.'

'No, it wasn't like that, Dave,' Babs insisted, but didn't have the chance to say any more just then because at that moment there was a *rat-tat* on the door and in walked Cedric Chivers, perhaps *alias* Gumby, in person!

A large maroon bow-tie now replaced his cravat and he was smoking a mini-cigar with something of a flourish.

'Ma's busy dolling herself up to go to the Ferry Inn,' he said, 'so I've taken the chance to slip back to have another palaver.'

'Oh, yes?' Dave's tone was dull, almost as though he couldn't take any more of Cedric's foppish ways and flippant chatter.

'No need to look so down-hearted, chummies,' Cedric breezed. 'Mister Fix-it, that's me. Yeah, I've talked Ma round and you and the ponies can stay.'

'Yippeee!' whooped Robin. 'Thanks a lot.'

'Wait a minute,' Cedric cautioned. 'Not so fast. Let me explain. In business circles I'm also known as Mister Ten per cent——'

'The tycoon type!' groaned Dave. 'I thought as much when you came in flourishing that cigar to impress us. Well, we're in a tight corner and you know it, so what's your proposition?'

50

'You're bang on the bull's eye—a fellow after my own heart.' Cedric slapped Dave on the back. 'So you'll appreciate that I'm letting you off lightly. Just give us ten per cent of your pony takings. That's the cut for Ma and me.'

'And for ten per cent you'll really let us and the ponies stay here for the rest of the summer?' Felicity prompted.

'Sure thing, bright-eyes.' Cedric inhaled on his cheroot. 'I'm easy as long as the lolly's there. Mind you, you'll have to keep Ma sweet.'

'And how do we do that?' asked Babs.

'By seeing that she gets a proper holiday here, same as my Aunty said she would . . . A nice, lazy time. No cleaning out of the cottages or changing the beds.'

He broke off as his mother's voice boomed from the path outside.

'Cedric! I'm ready and waiting.'

'No need for you to say "yes" to my proposition, chummies,' Cedric said as he moved to the door. 'You'll have to agree.' He smirked infuriatingly. 'Being in a tight spot, you've got no choice, have you?'

'You haven't finished yet, you know.'

Mrs Chivers blocked the passage as I went to put away my scrubbing brush and bucket next day, which happened to be a Saturday, change-over day for the holiday cottages.

'I've just been to inspect Number Five. The kitchen floor won't do,' Mrs Chivers added. 'That young Robin's skimped the corners. Then there are the cupboards. I distinctly told him to wipe out all the shelves and put in fresh paper.'

'He's only nine,' I protested, 'and he has got a sprained ankle.'

'I daresay,' Mrs Chivers said unsympathetically. 'He tried to tell me he was also developing house-maid's knee through too much scrubbing. You'll have to chase him up or do it yourself. I can't stand around any longer. I'm on holiday. I'm going to sit in the sun.'

Wearily we scrubbed on, house-bound, while,

outside, gulls were wheeling, terns diving in the greeny-blue sea, and yellow butterflies were fluttering over the tiny hearts-ease pansie in the sandhills.

Even more tantalising was the sight of our ponies. We'd had to tether them, because, when they'd heard the rattle of our buckets, they had come across to the cottages, hoping for food.

Dougal had managed to nose open one of the gates and had walked into the sitting room of Mariners' Cottage, leaving hoof-prints all over Felicity's newly-scrubbed tiles.

So there the ponies were, tied to the fence, while, from time-to-time, children fussed and fed them. New arrivals drooled over them and gave them yet more tit-bits—sweets, bars of chocolate, biscuits, stale sandwiches, and other unsuitable food.

Babs and I felt we couldn't stand by and let the ponies be ruined by having their tempers spoiled or being made ill.

Despite the fact that Mrs Chivers was watching us from her deck-chair, we hurriedly searched for some wood and made a notice-board.

'Let's hope that will do the trick.' Babs stood back to read the lettering which we had printed, with a felt pen, on to some cardboard which we nailed on the board. We knocked the notice-board into the ground beside the ponies.

PLEASE DO NOT FEED OR FUSS THE PONIES
RIDES ON THE BEACH LATER TODAY

'Babs! Jackie!' We flinched at the sound of Mrs Chivers's voice as she called to us from the garden of the cottage which she shared with Cedric. 'It's time you were back on the job. You've been fiddling with those ponies for fifteen minutes already. Your hammering's going through my head.'

We turned to obey her summons but, at that moment, there was a crash as the board fell against a boulder. Dougal, half-turning to edge his quarters against the notice, had used it as a scratching-post.

'Shetland mischief again!' sighed Babs, turning to pick up the sign.

'Jackie! The new people are arriving at Number Two,' Mrs Chivers shouted now. 'They'll want to unpack. Have you put new paper in the drawers?'

'Coming, Mrs Chivers!' I called and happened to catch the eye of a girl of about fourteen who had evidently just arrived. 'Never a dull moment!'

'Don't I know it,' sympathised the girl. 'I've got two ponies of my own at home. Let me lend a hand. I'll put the notice up a bit farther away from the ponies where they can't get at it.'

Babs and I went back to our chores, passing Dave on the way who was staggering under a load of groceries.

'There'll be another lot on the next ferry,' Cedric called after him. 'See you back on the jetty in an hour, chummy.'

Ten minutes later Babs and I were helping

Felicity to finish off Beach Cottage, and Dave was giving Robin a hand to sweep sand from the path. We were shaking the rugs outside when he saw Cedric settle in the deck-chair beside his mother in their garden. Tweetie was at their feet. They were tucking into what looked like bowls of strawberries and cream, while beside them on the table was a large plateful of scones and a pot of honey.

'Lucky things!' Babs sighed enviously. 'Look at them, tucking into an early tea while we're working like slaves.'

'Ah, well, we're nearly finished,' I said. 'Only one more cottage to clean and then we can go down to the beach.'

I spoke too soon. Pony-owners' work is never done! Next moment there was pandemonium from the tethered ponies. Misty was whinnying; Dougal squealing and Havoc, Patch and Moonlight were plunging and trying to pull away from the fence.

We ran to see what was happening. There was the sound of splintering wood, and, next moment, the ponies were running amok. Pieces of broken fencing banged against their legs, increasing their fright.

Meanwhile the cause of the upset zoomed past them in a buzzing drone.

'Panic stations!' Dave shouted. 'A swarm of bees!'

CHAPTER EIGHT

BEES AND BOTHER

It was heartless of us to laugh, but we just couldn't help it.

After the bees left the ponies, with their queen in the lead, they seemed to make for the Chivers's garden.

I don't know whether the queen had caught the scent of the honey and that was what influenced her, but she made a bee-line (sorry about the pun!) for the table where the Chiverses were having tea.

At the first sight of the swarm, Mrs Chivers jumped to her feet with a shriek. Cedric tried to flap bees away with his handkerchief, but, disregarding him, they flocked like a squadron of RAF bombers for the chair which his mother had vacated. The queen bee had already settled there and the others flocked around to keep her warm.

As the buzzing increased, Mrs Chivers, still shrieking and with flailing arms, ran indoors. She slammed the front door to keep out the swarm, and, in doing so, managed to shut out Cedric and Tweetie, who had to retreat round the side of the cottage and get in by the back door.

'D-d-d-don't l-l-let them see us laughing,' Babs choked, trying to hide her mirth. 'That would bring reprisals from Mrs C. for sure!'

We kept a watchful look-out for the bees while we sorted out the pony-bother. Patch was half-way down the path, with a piece of fencing dangling from his bridle. Babs raced after him, while Felicity and I ran to cope with Misty and Moonlight who had somehow got themselves tethered to each other by the same piece of broken fencing.

Havoc, true to his name, had dragged a fence post with him as he bolted into the Chivers's store-shed. The post had stuck cross-wise over the door, and the black pony could neither go right in, nor turn and come out again.

'Dougal,' Robin begged. 'Come back, you chump!'

He limped after the Shetland who—not wanting to be separated from his pony pal, even in a moment of disaster—was trying to force his way under the broken posts that had wedged crosswise against the door-frame. He wanted to join Havoc inside. Leaving Misty and Moonlight to Felicity, Dave and I ran to help Robin as we heard Havoc try to kick his way out by demolishing the side of the shed.

'Steady, Havoc!' Dave urged. 'Come back, Dougal. You'll wreck the shed between you.'

The wooden structure was already swaying on its foundations as I helped Robin to tug Dougal away, while Dave released the slip-knot that was

tethering Havoc to the broken fence post. He lifted the piece of wood aside, and Havoc came snorting out.

Wild-eyed in his distress, the black gelding wanted the comfort of Dougal's nearness.

'Look out!' came a warning from Babs as she hurried back on the scene, leading Patch. 'The bees are getting ready to swarm again.'

We looked towards the cottage to see Cedric and Mrs Chivers and Tweetie watching the drama from the shut windows. The bees were taking off again. They were now circling above the chair and seemed to be mustering in formation for some other venue.

'Help!' Felicity called. 'They're coming this way.'

'No, they're not,' said Robin as the bees changed course. 'Yes, they are. They're zig-zagging.'

The *zzzing* grew louder and I put my hands over my face in fright. Then the buzzing seemed to fade. I peeped through my fingers.

'Oh, thank goodness!' I gasped.

I sighed with relief as I saw the cloud of bees turning away, to follow their queen who, for some reason seemed to be making for a tree a hundred metres away.

'What I can't understand,' said Dave, when we were down on the beach with the ponies later, 'is how the fence came to break up so easily. We've tied the ponies up there before and it always seemed firm enough. In fact, I'd deliberately tested the posts.'

'Another mystery!' Felicity exclaimed. 'But this is one that I can solve. It was no accident. Cedric Gumby, or Chivers as he prefers to be known, deliberately shook and worked at the fencing until it came loose.'

'How can you possibly know that?' Dave asked sceptically.

'Because I saw him.' Felicity declared. 'I was at the upstairs window of our cottage. Cedric didn't know that anyone was around. I'd gone back to get a hankie.'

'I can believe it,' put in Babs. 'It all fits in. The Chiverses know that we suspect them because of my having seen them at the Marston Post Office and hearing them ask for letters in the name of Gumby. They must be planning something really crooked that's going to earn them a lot of money. So they're prepared to use any means to get us off the island so that we don't queer their pitch.'

'Yes,' I said emphatically, convinced that Babs' and Felicity's suspicions were correct, 'they won't stop at loosening fence posts. I bet they'll be doing even more drastic things to get rid of us. We'll have to be on our guard all the time.'

'Bosh!' said Dave. 'Cedric was probably just wiggling the posts because he hadn't anything better to do. It's the kind of loutish, vandalistic trick that any witless layabout would get up to. Anyway, Felicity——' he turned to his sister, 'what you saw can't really have made much impression on you at the time, otherwise you'd have told us before we tied the ponies up there.'

'I suppose I forgot, or hoped for the best,' Felicity said lamely.

'Quite,' said Dave. 'Anyway, I vote we stop letting our imaginations run away with us and get on with the job in hand. Here come the next lot of holidaymakers from the ferry. Come on now. Action stations!'

'Two pounds, eighty,' Dave said, adding up the takings after supper that night. 'Not bad when you consider that we had to spend most of the day in slave-labour, cleaning out the cottages for the Chiverses.'

'Not so good, though, after we've taken off the ten per cent for Mr Fix-it,' Felicity sighed.

'Ah, well, we've got a roof over our heads and the ponies are safe for the summer at any rate,' said Dave. 'But I must say the Chivers have put a blight on everything.' He looked at Robin. 'As well as all the other jobs, you and I will have to get busy with hammer and nails and mend the fence and the shed.'

There was a knock at the door before he had finished speaking and, as he opened it, we saw a girl standing there. She was Valerie, the friendly pony-girl who had helped Babs and me to put up the notice about not feeding the ponies that afternoon.

'Come right in,' Felicity invited. 'Thank heavens for a friendly face!'

'I wondered whether you'd consider letting me and my three friends hire four ponies for the day tomorrow, so that we could explore the island?' Valerie asked, smiling. 'We're all pony-owners and members of the Pony Club, so I can promise that your ponies will be in good hands. We'd gladly pay one pound fifty each for the day.'

'A total of six pounds!' whooped Robin. 'That would be a record.'

Dave was business-like. 'We'll have the ponies ready by nine o'clock tomorrow, Valerie. Will that suit you?'

'Great!'

When Babs and I were getting ready for bed she turned to me as the lighthouse beam flashed on the window pane.

'The day's turned out quite well after all,' she decided. 'Bees and bother, but—lots of lolly, too! I suppose you haven't found your Lucky Horseshoe, Jackie, by any chance?'

I shook my head. I didn't want to be a blight, but I couldn't help feeling that our little bit of good luck couldn't last for long.

And, of course, I was right!

'Mind your p's and q's today,' Felicity warned next morning after Babs and I had helped her to get the four ponies ready for Valerie and her friends while Dave and Robin were busy with hammer and nails repairing the damaged fence and shed. 'Dave's in one of his moods.'

'Big brothers!' Babs said feelingly. 'And to

think I used to be sorry for myself because I was an only child! What's upset Dave today?'

'You and Jackie, I'm afraid,' Felicity said apologetically. 'I heard him muttering something about pony-girls always being a blight. That was after he hit his thumb with the hammer. You see, he blames you and Jackie for tying the ponies to the fence. He said you ought to have had more sense.'

'He's right,' I confessed. 'It was my idea—not Felicity's. Do you think I ought to go and tell Dave I'm sorry?'

'Oh, no,' Felicity said quickly. 'The best way to please him when he's in one of these moods is to keep right out of the way.'

'So we'd probably be doing him a favour if we went off for the day,' Babs said. 'Brainwave! There are lots of sausages in the fridge, so we could take them to Smuggler's Cove and join up with Valerie and her friends for a Sausage Sizzle.'

Meanwhile Dave and Robin had gone out of sight, probably to get some more timber from the yard behind the Chivers's cottage.

'Now's our chance,' said Babs. 'Come on.'

We loaded frying pans and food into the saddle-bags, strapped them on to Dougal and set off across Pony Island.

As we came in sight of the cove we saw Valerie and her friends riding the ponies through the sunlit shallows at the sea's edge. It made a super holiday picture—the four ponies, black, bay, skewbald and grey, with their girl-riders in jeans and gaily-coloured shirts; the sparkling sea, the white-topped waves and the wheeling gulls.

Babs jumped on to a rock and cupped her hands to shout to them : 'Coo-eee!'

We saw one of the girls look round and say something to the others. Then they all waved.

At the same moment, Dougal sighted Havoc. He whinnied to his pony-pal, and started to pull. Havoc neighed back. Taking Felicity by surprise, Dougal reared and then broke into a canter, dragging his reins from Felicity's hands. We all three ran after him. Dougal started to gallop, full-speed towards his pal.

Havoc's rider—a fair-haired girl called Lynne —also seemed to be having difficulty. We saw Havoc wheel and try to pull away as if he wanted to leave the water and come to meet Dougal. The girl seemed determined not to let him have his wilful way. She gave the black a flip with the reins and drove him on with her calves through the shallows.

Havoc, however, was not going to be so easily defeated. He dug in his toes, and refused to budge.

'Oh, no!' Babs gasped as Havoc seemed to pause and then deliberately went down on his elbows. 'He's going to roll.'

We watched in dismay as Havoc's big bulk flopped into the water. Lynn jumped clear just in time, but she was up to her waist in the waves before she could struggle to her feet.

We saw Valerie and the other two girls rein

up their ponies and look back to see what was the matter. Then Lynne hauled Havoc to his feet and scolded him as she led him towards the beach.

At that moment, Dougal reached the scene.

'Dougal won't go in the sea,' Felicity predicted. 'That's for sure. He hates getting his feet wet.'

However, in his eagerness to join his friend, Havoc, Dougal, for once, forgot his fear. Whinnying, he splashed through the wavelets towards the black whom Lynne was now leading ashore.

Dougal sent the spray up in a rainbow-shower. The Shetland's legs were shorter than Havoc's, and the breaking waves seemed to catch him on the flanks.

We could see that Dougal was almost being knocked off his balance. Then he seemed to put his foot into a hollow, and, next moment, he was down.

Snorting and whinnying, he panicked as he remembered his worst fears. Not only had he got his feet wet, but he was well and truly in the water—wet all over, and also wetting the saddle-bags containing the food!

'The sausages!' groaned Babs, breaking into a run. 'They'll be ruined.'

'The bread will be salty, too,' I sighed as I sped to the rescue. I passed the dripping Lynne, and astonished Valerie, Sheila and Kathie and I gasped: 'We planned such a super Sausage

c

Sizzle for you! I love ponies, but they're certainly spelling trouble this summer!'

'Too true,' sighed Babs as she met my gaze. 'What worries me is what Dave's going to say when he hears about this, and we needn't kid ourselves that he won't find out because a saddle as wet as Dougal's will take some explaining.'

CHAPTER NINE

'PLEASE SAVE MY PONY!'

'Well, that didn't taste too bad,' said Valerie some time later, as we finished the moistly-fried sausages. 'At least they didn't need any extra salt.'

Then, about an hour afterwards, Lynne—who had changed into a swimsuit—decided that her clothes were dry enough to wear.

'Perhaps we ought to make a move,' she suggested. 'We've still got some more of the island to explore.'

'We'll come with you as far as the Shadow Pony rocks,' offered Babs.

So, with the girls riding, and Felicity, Babs and I walking alongside, leading Dougal, we climbed up the cliff path, and cut across the turf towards the mound of rocks.

We'd gone about three hundred metres when we heard a roar of motor-bike engines. Next moment three leather-jacketed youths came bouncing over the grass.

Babs gesticulated to warn them away from the ponies, but the youths deliberately switched course and came straight towards us, revving their engines menacingly.

Havoc shied, Patch reared, and Moonlight and Misty began to buck. Dougal kicked up his heels, and wriggled out of his bridle before setting off at a canter for home.

At the same moment, Dave and Robin, having several minutes earlier seen the approach of the motor cyclists, came running over the turf.

'Hey, look out!' Dave shouted to the youths. 'You're upsetting the ponies.'

Laughing tauntingly, the youths circled round us, and one of them, with straggly fair hair and his name EDDIE in studs across his leather jacket, stopped within two metres of the terrified Moonlight.

'There's more 'orse-power in me bike than in ten of them 'orses of yours,' Eddie jeered. He opened the throttle to make his engine roar again. 'Why don't you get really mobile, and do a ton, like this?'

Just then, to our relief, there sounded the clang of the bell from the causeway, warning visitors to the island that the roadway would soon be submerged by the tide.

'Wot a shime!' Eddie mocked. 'Just when we were going to have a bit of fun and a wild west rodeo with your broncs.'

'Over my dead body,' Dave said grimly.

'Hark at big boy! Trying to put the frighteners on us,' Eddie laughed. 'We'll see you lot again.'

'Ta-ta for now,' said another youth. He turned his machine to race away. 'We'll be back, and we'll bring all our pals next time. We'll be mob-handed!'

We tried not to think about the youths' dire threat, hoping that we might never see Eddie and his gang again.

How wrong we were!

Meanwhile we had to face Dave's disapproval when we got back to the cottages.

'You ought to have had more sense, the three of you,' he declared, taking off Dougal's sopping saddle. 'Sloping off for the day as soon as my back was turned, without a word. And as for taking Dougal, you might have known there'd be trouble as soon as he caught sight of Havoc.'

'That was it,' Babs sighed. 'If that Shetland hasn't seen his pal for a couple of hours, there has to be a wild reunion.'

'Who would have thought Dougal would plunge into the waves to join Havoc when Lynne was riding through the water?' I said. 'Dougal's supposed to hate water.'

'That Shetland's capable of anything,' Dave

said. 'He's a menace. And so are pony-girls.' He glared at Babs and me. 'Well, this saddle's going to take a couple of days to dry out. Then there'll be all the leatherwork to be cleaned. So you and your cousin are going to be busy, Jackie.'

'Very well, Dave,' I said, and added unhappily; 'You seem convinced that Babs and I are a couple of flops.'

'No, I don't.' Dave gave me a sudden smile. 'You're very good at one thing——'

'What's that?' Babs asked brightening.

'You're better than Felicity at rustling up good nosh.' Dave sounded almost light-hearted. 'So please get cracking in the kitchen now, if you don't mind. All Robin and I have had since breakfast is a choc bar. The only thing that's kept me going has been the prospect of my favourite high tea—sausage and mash!'

Babs and I looked at each other in dismay.

'This is terrible!' Babs said feelingly before whispering to me: 'You tell him, Jackie, I daren't.'

Dave wilted with disappointment as I explained how all the sausages had been eaten at the Sausage Sizzle and how in the excitement of getting ready for the picnic, we'd forgotten to restock with supplies.

'The best we can offer you,' confessed Babs, 'is bread fried in bacon fat, and half a jar of jam!'

'Ugh!' Dave grimaced. 'Pony-girls! If ever a fellow suffered! Why couldn't you have stuck to your pony-clubs, gymkhanas and jolly mucking-out and left me in peace? Why did you have to come to Pony Island?'

'Wake up, Jackie!'

Babs was shaking me as moonlight flooded the bedroom. From outside I could hear the stamping of hooves, a protesting whinny and

then a crash, followed by Dave's and Robin's voices.

'Something's wrong with the ponies,' I gasped. 'Not yet more pony-trouble! There's no end to it.'

I jumped out of bed, pulled on my jeans and sweater, thrust my feet into my gumboots and ran downstairs. On our way to the back door we bumped into Felicity who had also heard the commotion.

71

Picking up the storm torch from the table, we hurried on to the hillside to see the boys' collapsed tent with Dave and Robin struggling from under the canvas, while, nearby, stood the cause of the trouble—Dougal!

The Shetland's eyes were wild in the moonlight. He was kicking at his stomach, moving restlessly and lurching as if he didn't know what to do with himself.

'Colic,' diagnosed Babs in dismay. 'He's threshing about because of the pain. That's how he knocked the tent down.'

'Quick!' Dave crawled from under the canvas and ran to grasp Dougal's headstall. 'Go to the other side of him, Robin. We mustn't let him get down, or he might roll and twist his gut.'

'What do you think caused the colic?' Felicity asked.

'I should think it's obvious,' Dave groaned. 'You three are to blame. He got a chill from his ducking and he might have swallowed some sand.'

'We ought to get him under cover,' I said, 'in a narrow space, if possible, where he can't lie down. Then we could put a hot blanket round him. That's what the vet advised once when Misty had colic.'

'The Chivers's shed!' exclaimed Babs. 'The very place. We'll have to use it. This could be a matter of life and death.'

'And we've *got* to get the vet,' decided Dave. 'There are no two ways about it. We haven't got

72

any colic-drench here, or any means of making any. Dougal will need an injection.' He turned to me as Dougal started 'hoofing' again at his own stomach. The pony's breathing was now laboured, and his flanks were sweaty. 'I can't leave him, Jackie. You go and 'phone the nearest vet while the rest of us try to get him into the shed.'

'Where's the telephone?' I asked.

'There's only one,' Dave looked desperate. 'At the Chiverses!'

'Sorry, Jackie,' Robin called after me. 'Do your best.'

My heart was thumping as I ran to the Chivers's cottage. The thought of Mrs Chivers's rage at my waking them up at two o'clock in the morning made me shudder. All the same I had to do it. Dougal's life depended on it.

I hammered with both fists on the door, and, almost immediately, Tweetie began to bark as he scrabbled at the other side. An upstairs window was flung open and Cedric's pained voice demanded:

'What's wrong? Waking people up at two in the morning! And why are you putting a pony in that shed?'

'I'm sorry to disturb you,' I shouted above Tweetie's barks. 'It's an emergency. Dougal's been taken ill. He needs the vet. It's a matter of life and death. Please, please let me use your telephone.'

CHAPTER TEN

PAYING THE PRICE

'Keep the pony warm and don't let him lie down,' the vet advised over the telephone. 'I'll be at the Ferry Inn jetty in twenty minutes. If the causeway's awash, please have a boat to meet me.'

A boat! My mind whirled as I heard the telephone click at the other end. I glanced out of the window to see moonlight silvering the sea. One look at the beach and I saw that the tide was high. Twenty minutes! There wasn't much time to lose, and how was I going to get a boat?

I dashed to ask Cedric who was now wearing a striped, velveteen dressing gown over scarlet pyjamas.

'Oh, dear. You'll need to borrow the outboard,' he said, with a tired yawn. 'It's in the back kitchen. Aunty's dinghy is the blue one, down on the beach.'

'Oh, thank you, Cedric,' I gasped. 'That's absolutely super of you.'

Wide-awake now, Cedric's eyes took on a greedy gleam. 'It'll cost you,' he announced, smoothing down his sleek fair hair which had become ruffled in the draught from the door 'Two pounds,' he bargained.

74

'Highway robbery!' I protested.

'No money—no outboard!' Cedric said definitely.

'Oh, very well,' I was forced to agree, 'but don't ask Dave for it. Babs and I'll pay for it from our pocket-money.'

Meanwhile the others had been busy. As I left the Chivers's cottage, I met Babs and Felicity carrying a blanket that they had soaked in hot water.

We went towards the shed where Robin and Dave were waiting with Dougal, and I was aware of two pairs of eyes watching us from the upstairs window of the Chivers's cottage. Babs must have sensed them, too, because without saying anything to each other, we both turned and saw, in the moonlight, the tense black head of Tweetie at the window. Above him Mrs Chivers was bulging from a frothy nightgown, the outline of her hair made irregular by horn-like rollers.

'I bet she's seething,' Babs said forebodingly. 'I wish she'd go back to bed. She's sure to be in a filthy temper tomorrow.'

There wasn't room for us all in the shed with Dougal, so Babs handed the steaming blanket to Felicity and Robin who held it under the pony's stomach while Dave humped the outboard over the shingle to the beach.

The Shetland rolled his eyes and slightly turned his head as if trying to see what Felicity and Robin were doing. Then the warmth of the blanket seemed to comfort him. All the same, his

75

breathing was noisy, so I made a pad of dried grass and wiped the sweat from his flanks.

It seemed an age before we heard the footfalls of Dave and the vet.

With a powerful torch the vet examined Dougal. Then he took his temperature. We waited tensely while he read the thermometer. I remembered a first-aid talk at the Pony Club when we had been told that a very high temperature, in the case of colic, would indicate a twisted gut. In severe cases the pony had to be shot. Was that to be Dougal's fate?

We watched the vet's expression as he gazed at the mercury.

'A hundred and two,' he said before shaking it down. 'Bad enough, but I don't think there's a twist: I'll give him an injection. Together with your hot-blanket treatment, it should relax the gut.' He looked across at Dave. 'Well, I think the younger ones could go back to bed now, don't you? I'll hang on for a while to see how Dougal goes on; then perhaps you'll be good enough to take me back to the mainland, David.'

As we trudged back to the cottage, Robin hobbled beside me.

'Dougal will probably recover, but I'll never be able to sell him.' Robin sounded sad. 'Other people won't understand about his dislike of getting wet. At some time or other they'd make him go through a stream or into the sea. Then he'd throw them off and probably end up with another attack of colic.'

76

'Yes,' sighed Felicity, 'and how would he get on without Havoc?'

'Or Havoc without him?' said Robin.

'Oh, dear!' sighed Babs. 'It could be one of those unsolvable pony-problems.'

'Solved only by a bullet, I suppose,' Robin said quietly. 'I couldn't bear that. Oh, poor Dougal!'

Just then the moon came from behind the clouds. The moonbeams struck the rocks on the hilltop at just the right angle because, clearly thrown on the moon-lit turf, was the outline of the galloping Shadow Pony.

We stopped to gaze in wonder.

'That's the first time we've seen the Shadow Pony by moonlight,' said Felicity.

'It could be an omen,' said Babs.

'Yes.' Robin wouldn't be comforted. 'Perhaps a bad one!'

We scrambled out of bed early next day despite the fact that we had been up half the night.

Already Dave and Robin had been attending to Dougal. They had found him looking slightly better; his eyes were less inflamed and he was breathing more easily. So Dave had given him a bucket of warm water, and now he and Robin were leading him gently around.

'He's bound to feel a bit frail for a few days,' Dave said. 'So I suppose we'll have to use the shed as a stable and hope that the Chiverses won't mind. We can picket him outside for part of the day, but we can't let him roam round loose in case he eats something that might upset him again.'

I went to get the pony-nuts that we took down to the beach to give the animals a midday snack. To my surprise the bucket had already been partly filled from the sack. I was about to scoop in some more when I noticed that the nuts already in the bucket had a gritty look. I ran my finger over them and detected grains of sand.

Sand in the pony-nuts, I thought. Somebody must have been very careless.

I called to the others: 'Have any of you had sand in this bucket?'

'Sand in a pony-feed bucket!' echoed Dave. 'Of course not. We'd have had to be out of our minds. Even a few grains of sand in his feed would give a pony colic.'

'Well, someone put sand in the bucket,' I insisted. 'Look! And if it wasn't any of us, who was it?'

'The same person who loosened the fence-posts,' declared Babs. 'Cedric Chivers!'

'More wild accusations!' Dave said, exasperatedly. 'We'll nail this once and for all. The sand is undoubtedly what caused Dougal's colic, but why should we jump to the conclusion that Cedric's responsible?'

'Because he's a creep,' put in Robin.

'I daresay, but that doesn't necessarily mean he'd go to these lengths. Anyway, he's over there in the garden, setting up his deck-chair, I'll go and get him.'

A moment later Dave came back with Cedric who was looking both sullen and puzzled.

To our amazement Cedric gazed down into the bucket and suddenly looked contrite. 'Yes, I did give Dougal some pony-nuts and I daresay I was seen doing it—and why not? I only thought I was cheering him up. It was after he'd got back from his wetting. He was standing there looking the picture of misery. I didn't notice any sand in

the bucket. Someone else must have put it there, probably some kids were playing around. But it just shows that this is no place for your ponies. Something really terrible might happen to them. So why don't you all pack it in and clear off? You could all stay at Jackie's place.'

Babs exploded with indignation. 'Neither you nor anyone else is going to make us leave Pony Island.'

'That's right,' confirmed Dave. He looked sternly at Cedric. 'We're giving you the benefit of the doubt over this. But if we find that you get up to any tricks to upset our ponies, we'll sort you out in a way that you won't like. So, watch it, chum.'

We spent most of the day giving pony-rides on the beach although we were short-handed be-

cause Robin stayed with Dougal for part of the time.

Business was still brisk even at five o'clock in the afternoon—when it usually tailed off—so I told the others to carry on while I went up to Seashell Cottage to cut some sandwiches and mix some lemonade.

'Hurrah, eats!' exclaimed Robin as I took his share to where he was sitting on the turf near Dougal who was now beginning to graze. 'I'm starving.'

'So am I.' I sat down beside him. 'I'll eat mine here and keep you company.'

Robin and I munched companionably while the red-spotted Burnet moths alighted on a pink-starred clump of thyme nearby. It was peaceful in the August sunshine.

Down on the beach, grown-ups sat in deck-chairs, children paddled, or built sandcastles and the ponies, a little tired now, ambled up and down with their riders. Even Tweetie, for the moment, was at peace. Instead of barking from the window of the Chivers's cottage, he was curled up, nose on paws, asleep on the window-seat.

Suddenly the serene mood was shattered. From the mainland came the roar of open-throttled motor-bike engines. Robin and I looked at each other in alarm. So the vandals were back! We ran to the top of the rocky hillock and stared across the sound to the mainland.

There, by the Ferry Inn jetty, were nine leather-jacketed youths, serpentining their motor-bikes down the curving road to the causeway—just what I'd been dreading!

The tide was ebbing but there was still several centimetres of water over the cobbles.

'This is terrible,' Robin groaned in despair. 'In a few minutes, they'll have splashed across the causeway and zoomed up the track here. Then they'll start riding round and round Dougal, upsetting him. The shock could bring back his colic, and perhaps finish him off. What are we going to do, Jackie?'

'Oh, gosh, I just don't know!' I looked round in panic. 'We might put him in the shed, shut the door and stand guard over him.'

'Too late!' Robin gazed across at the mainland where the ton-up boys were astride their bikes by the lapping causeway. 'They've seen us.'

The boys were pointing in our direction and jeering. We recognised one of them from their last visit—the one with his name in brass studs on his jacket—Eddie!

'We said we'd be back,' Eddie shouted to us. 'Get ready for the rodeo!'

I flung my arms protectingly round Dougal's neck. How could we save him? Robin and I were outnumbered nine to two, and the ton-up boys were all big and brutal—and horrible bullies!

CHAPTER ELEVEN

SHADOW PONY SHOCK

I watched in horror as Eddie revved up his bike to ride through the shallow water on the causeway.

He'd gone only a few metres when his wheels started to spin and his engine spluttered. He seemed to hesitate. Then he put his feet on the ground and, hastily turning his bike, moved it clear of the water.

Was he retreating? Could we dare to hope?

Robin and I crossed our fingers for luck as the youths talked among themselves. Eddie was pointing at the water swirling over the causeway. Was he wondering whether the tide was coming in or going out?

Then, to our amazement, we saw Cedric dash from behind a rock where he had been sunbathing and run towards the island side of the causeway.

'Come on, Eddie,' he yelled, beckoning them forward. 'It's O.K. Bring the gang across and give the pony-kids the frighteners. That's what you're here for.'

Robin and I exchanged dumbfounded glances. So Cedric and Eddie knew each other. They were in league, with the purpose of getting us off the island. Why? What was at stake for the Chiverses? It would have to be something big to justify them going to such lengths as to get the sinister co-operation of Eddie and his ton-up boys. We watched in dread as Eddie, after shouting something indistinguishable across to Cedric, conferred with the other youths. One of them was pointing to the water which was swirling over the causeway. Then Eddie shouted across to Cedric.

'Listen, Ced. We won't let you down. We'll come another time. We don't want to risk getting sea-water in the plugs. Next time, we'll judge the tide right and give the kids the full treatment. O.K.?'

This time, Dave just had to believe that the Chiverses were wanting to get us off the island.

'The thing that puzzles me,' said Dave, 'is that they seem to be going about it in such a sneaky round-about way—making us clean up the cottages, upsetting the ponies, insisting on ten per cent of our takings, Cedric getting Eddie to bring the ton-up boys here and encouraging them to torment us and the ponies. If the Chiverses are so keen to do all that to get rid of us, why don't they just tell us to go?'

'I suppose it might come to that,' I said unhappily. 'But if they did evict us, without really good cause, they would be breaking the contract.'

'That's right,' said Dave, 'and they probably

85

realise that, if they did that, Dad would get in touch with the Chiverses in Australia by air mail, and claim back the rent. My guess is that Cedric and his mother are trying to make us so fed up that we'll be only too glad to go of our own accord, and that's something we're not going to do!'

'Definitely not,' agreed Babs.

We nodded in agreement; all the same we knew that the danger time would be the following Saturday when we might hear the dreaded roar of their bikes as the ton-up boys swept over the causeway, intent on tormenting us and the ponies.

We decided we'd have to defend the island. So we spent a whole afternoon piling up big rocks at each side of the causeway. At the first sound of the leather boys approach we planned to gallop to the causeway and roll the rocks across to form a barricade. We knew that the boys could roll the ricks aside and still get through but we felt that our attempts might discourage them and that they would, perhaps, decide to zoom on elsewhere.

Mercifully, for that weekend at least, we were spared a visit from them.

Meanwhile Dougal grew stronger every day, and Robin's ankle was less painful so that he could now lead the ponies up and down the beach. Things seemed to be going better and

Dave, for the time being, was less critical of us. We understood him more than he realised. He was on edge because of worry over his family's homelessness and the need to earn the ponies' winter feed.

'I'm not as scared of Dave as I used to be,' I confided to Babs, 'and I still like him even when he does get impatient. Mind you, it's absolutely super when he's smiling and friendly. That's how he'd always be if he wasn't so worried.'

'Oh, you're too kind-hearted,' Babs said frankly. 'In my opinion, Dave's too big for his boots, as well as being thoroughly ungracious.'

I hadn't realised just how sensitive Babs was as regards what Dave thought of us. I think she really liked Dave a lot more than she would allow herself to admit. It was obvious a few days later that she was relieved and happy when Dave came back from the mainland with news that vindicated us.

'Full marks to you, Babs, and to you, Jackie!' he said wholeheartedly, as he sat down to supper. 'You were both right and I was wrong. Cedric and his Mum really have got a lot at stake. It's not just that they're mean-minded. I'm sure now that they're involved in something really crooked with a lot of money involved.'

'Why?' Felicity was wide-eyed. 'What have you discovered, Dave?'

'Well, when I went into the chemist's to get the embrocation for Havoc's tendon, the Chiverses were already in the shop. They couldn't see me because there was a pyramid of boxes of tissues between us.'

'What were they doing?' asked Babs, agog.

'I couldn't see what was happening,' said Dave, 'but I could hear what the chemist was saying and he sounded very surprised I must say; "Now let me get this clear, Mrs Chivers," he was confirming. "You want me to send off these negatives of the cottages to have fifty prints made of each. That'll be a total of three hundred altogether. Rather a big order, isn't it? It'll cost you quite a lot." '

'What did Mrs Chivers say to that?' Felicity prompted.

'She just said that she didn't mind what it cost her as long as she got the prints quickly,' Dave reported.

'Why do the Chiverses want all those photographs of the cottages?' I puzzled. 'The cottages don't even belong to them.'

'That's what I've been wondering,' said Dave. 'They might be trying to work some kind of a swindle, but I don't know what. This might explain the mystery that Babs stumbled on when she overheard them in the Marston Post Office. The Chiverses real name *could* be Gumby and they might have had their letters addressed to the post office at Marston because they couldn't very well have had them re-addressed here without the postman getting suspicious.'

'What ought we to do?' asked Robin. 'Go to the police?'

'I wonder.' Dave looked thoughtful. 'The Chiverses—or Gumbys—probably haven't committed any crime yet. So we haven't really got any evidence that would convince the police. I think the best thing would be to keep our eyes open and be careful not to let the Chiverses know that we've found out any more about them.'

Babs nodded. 'Just play it cool and do what Dave says.' She looked across at the older boy. 'Well done, Dave! I think you've discovered something really important, and it was jolly clever of you not to let the Chiverses know that you'd overheard about all those photographs.'

During the next week the weather was warm and sunny—ideal for holidaymakers and pony-riders.

An extra ferry boat brought yet more visitors to Pony Island. Many of them were busy with their cameras because, due to the bright sunlight, the Shadow Pony showed up exceptionally clearly, galloping across the turf. Down on the beach the children were queuing all morning for pony rides and we did record business.

At lunchtime we were able to have a break while the families and children had picnic lunches on the beach, or trooped back to their cottages.

I took off Misty's saddle, and, gathering some dried grass from the cliff-top, made a pad with which to rub her back. Since Patch had developed a saddle-sore earlier in the holidays, we'd been careful to make sure that the ponies did not have any further trouble.

Carrying riders of different weights—some of whom slumped heavily in the saddle—put a strain on the ponies, so we always made a point of resting them at lunchtime, removing their bits and saddles and rubbing their backs to help their circulation.

Misty, as always, loved this attention. She was bending her neck and turning her head round to nibble at my shirt as I wisped her.

'Oh, Misty, you are a fusspot!' I broke off to rub her between the eyes. 'You know that I adore you, and you revel in it.'

As my pony and I were in the middle of this love-scene a small girl came up to us, begging for a ride.

Felicity, kind-heartedly, jumped to her feet, tightened Moonlight's girths and led the child to the rocks and back.

'That's twenty-two times I've been up and down the sands today,' she said at last, helping down Moonlight's rider and pouring herself a glass of lemonade from the plastic container that we had taken down to the beach.

'That ought to buy a good lot of pony-nuts for the winter,' Robin said happily.

'It would,' agreed Dave, 'if it wasn't for the fact that Cedric had to have his cut. Do you realise, that out of every ten pounds we make, we have to give Cedric one?'

'The thought chokes me,' spluttered Felicity, 'especially as all he does with his money is to spend it on fancy clothes. Just look at him——'

We gazed across at Cedric. Wearing a terra-cotta towelling-shirt and matching stay-pressed slacks, he was strolling across the sands with a transistor blaring.

A few moments after Cedric had disappeared behind some rocks at the far end of the beach, a warning shriek from Babs made us suddenly alert.

'Oh, look!' she exclaimed, jumping to her feet. 'Something terrible's happening!'

Our eyes followed her indignantly-pointing finger towards the galloping Shadow Pony on the hillside.

I could hardly believe what I saw.

A figure appeared to be astride the pony, riding it. He was brandishing a stick as though to urge it over the turf.

It might have been a thrilling sight—a youth excitedly riding the famous pony, if he hadn't—at the same time—been actively destroying it. Right from the first moment that we glimpsed him, the youth was ruining the shadow. The swish of his heavy stick sent down the rock that caused the shadow of one ear. Then the other 'ear' rolled down the slope. Now he was crouching over the mane as, on the ridge, he dislodged one by one the stones that cast the shadow of the pony's neck.

I felt shocked as I saw that the youth was then

using a stake to lever away the rock which formed part of the mound that threw the shadow of the pony's head. I was sickened as the boulder hurtled down the slope—and suddenly the Shadow Pony was no more! It was just a shapeless blob.

Mercifully fate took over at that moment. A cloud came over the sun and the shadow faded.

'The end of the Shadow Pony.' Felicity sounded sad. 'How terrible!'

It had all happened so quickly. The damage was done before any of us could rush into action.

Leaving the ponies in the shade and telling Robin to take charge of the cash-table, Dave set off up the hillside at a run with Felicity, and Babs and I, behind him. The youth was now out of sight, but when we reached the top of the hill we saw him sprawled on the grass on the other side. It was Eddie—the ringleader of the ton-up, leather-boys. There he was, drinking coke from a tin, with his motor-bike propped against a rock nearby, and none of his gang around. Eddie must have decided to be a 'loner' for once.

'Hi!' he called as we panted up. 'You three look hot and bothered. Anything wrong?'

'I'll say there is,' Dave said angrily. 'In two minutes flat, you've destroyed something that's been here for hundreds of years—the island's Shadow Pony.'

'Shadow Pony?' Eddie put on a show of looking surprised. 'Never heard of it. What is it?'

As Babs explained, with interjections from

Dave and me, Eddie seemed to listen almost sympathetically.

'Well! well!' he said at last. 'It does seem that I've been naughty to roll down those rocks. Very naughty! So it's only right that I should make good the damage. Suppose I dump the stones back up the mound and, when the sun comes out, you and your pals can build up your Shadow Pony again—perhaps better than ever.'

We gazed at him in amazement. He must think that we were feeble-minded, we thought.

'You're not going to fool us,' I told him frankly. 'Robin and I were watching you when you brought your ton-up gang to the causeway and you and Cedric were calling across to each other. You pair are as close as a couple of thieves.'

'Smart, aren't you?' Eddie was only momentarily taken aback. 'But I didn't do what Cedric wanted, did I? We could have come across the causeway if we'd waited half an hour. The tide was going out.'

We looked at each other nonplussed. Could we possibly believe him?

'Ced wanted me to come again, last weekend,' Eddie pointed out, 'but I wasn't havin' any. Why persecute a few ponies an' a bunch of kids? That's what I said. S'matter of fact, that's why I've come by myself, today, hopin' I'd see you lot. I wanted to tell you that I was on your side.'

'A likely story,' Dave said sceptically.

'S'right. I'm not like the rest of the mob. I'm

93

not a real ton-upper, you know. Sometimes I'd rather be on my own.' He got to his feet and rolled up his sleeves with a show of business-like readiness. 'Now, to help you, eh, same as I said.'

Eddie was in a talkative mood and he went on chatting as he helped Dave and Babs and me to carry and roll the rocks back up the slope.

'Had a good season with your ponies, eh? Giving rides is a paying game, I bet. Well, the best of British luck to you . . . So you're 'ere for the summer holidays? . . . Nice work if you can get it . . . Is that your tent behind that cottage with all the seashells round the door? And was that your dog—the black one that disappeared over there?'

'Tweetie?' We looked round in surprise because we thought the Chivers had left him shut up in the cottage.

'Oh, he isn't there now,' Eddie told us. 'No good looking for him. It was earlier on that he scarpered.'

'What do you mean?' Babs looked at Eddie in alarm. If there was anything amiss with Tweetie we were sure to be blamed. 'Where is he? What happened to him?'

'He suddenly sprang from nowhere,' Eddie told us. 'Got in the way of one of the rolling rocks. It might have touched him, but I don't think so. He went yelping that a-way.' He jerked his thumb towards the ruined castle. 'Tell you what, chummies. You go after him and make sure he's all right. I'll carry on building up the rest of these stones. I'll make a real job of it. Trust me! Honest Eddie, that's me. I wouldn't fool you.'

CHAPTER TWELVE

A TERRIBLE DISCOVERY

Trust Eddie—that's the last thing we ought to have done!

Thinking that Tweetie might have been hurt by the rolling rock and be lying injured somewhere, we spent the best part of an hour looking for him, but without any luck. So we decided to go back to the beach, collect the ponies, and mount a full-scale search.

Even while we were hunting for the Chivers's dog I felt somehow uneasy about Eddie. It was his glib 'Trust me' which made me wonder. Had he been trying to get us off the scene for some reason? And if so, why?

What was his game?

It was with these uneasy thoughts that I joined the others in quartering the island.

'Tweetie! *Tweetie!*'

On the other side of the hill, Felicity and Dave were also searching. Meanwhile Cedric appeared on the scene.

'Ma'll go mad if Tweetie isn't found!' he groaned. 'She's gone off to the mainland to have a hair-do, and she said I wasn't to let Tweetie out of the cottage. I can't think how he got out. I must have left the door open when I went for my transistor. If we don't find him before Ma gets back, she'll go bonkers. She thinks more of that dog than she does of me.'

So there was Cedric, poking a stick into clumps of brambles and, at the same time, trying to keep himself clear of the prickles so as not to pull the threads of his fancy towelling shirt.

Suddenly, above the thud of Misty's hoof-beats, I thought I heard a whimper. I reined up to listen, and realised the sound was coming from a sandy bank where there was a rabbit warren. I dismounted and, calling to the others, led Misty to the scene. As I neared the warren, the whimper became a plaintive whine.

'Are you there, Tweetie?' I called.

There came a muffled yap in reply. I gazed round at the rabbit holes and gorse. Then, in one of the big holes, where part of the bank had caved in, I saw a dark shape moving.

I hurried across to see the tip of Tweetie's tail. The rest of him was hidden by a boulder which must have fallen across the entrance to the burrow.

'Keep still, Tweetie. Good dog!' I encouraged as I tugged at the stone. It was too heavy and big for me to move.

'Cedric! Dave!' I called. 'Come and help.'

To my relief Dave came galloping on to the scene.

'Thank goodness!' I gasped as he slid down

D

from Havoc and raced to my aid. 'Someone strong is needed to move this boulder.'

A few moments later Dave was examining the freed Tweetie, while Cedric panted up the last few metres of the slope.

'Gosh, what a mess he's in!' Cedric exclaimed, gazing in horror at the dog who, sand clogging

his burr-covered coat, was wriggling happily in Dave's arms delighted to be free. 'You'll have to carry him down for me, Dave. I bought this gear only last Saturday, and I don't want to get it spoiled.'

Back at the Chivers's cottage, Dave put Tweetie inside and firmly shut the door while Cedric, smoothing his hair, went to meet his mother whose pink dress and dyed blonde hair was visible as she waddled up the hill from the jetty.

'Well, that's that,' Dave declared, stretching himself. 'Now to get back to our cottage, Jackie. I didn't like the way Eddie questioned us. Very fishy! We've got more than a hundred and fifty pounds in pony-ride takings under that loose floorboard, and we haven't even bothered to lock the front door.'

'You're right.' I gazed at him in horror. 'We've got to hurry.'

Trust me! Trust me! *Trust me!* Eddie's words seemed to echo in my brain as I hurried after Dave to Seashell Cottage. Now we were in a panic as we realised how Eddie could have fooled us.

Felicity, Babs and Robin were close behind as Dave hurried up the narrow stairs. Frantically, he pulled up the loose floorboard under which we kept the takings. As we had feared, there was nothing there.

'Just as I thought,' Dave groaned. 'But however did Eddie find it?'

'I suppose a thief knows all the hiding places,' said Babs.

'All these weeks of hard work for nothing!' sighed Felicity. 'Now there'll be no winter keep for the ponies and we'll have to get rid of them.'

'We can't,' Robin resolved. 'We've got to stop Eddie. He can't have gone far.'

'Come on,' I urged. 'If we get the ponies we might be able to catch him.'

Dave was already half-way down the stairs. 'There's no time to lose,' he urged. 'And there's one hopeful sign. The tide's over the causeway so he won't be able to ride across on his motor-bike!'

We must have looked a wild posse as we leaped on to our ponies and galloped across the turf, heading for the ferry-jetty.

As we reached the ridge from which the land fell away to the Sound we saw Eddie, the sole passenger, in the returning ferry. He was sitting in the stern, his motor-bike propped against the gunwale. Old Ben, the ferryman, was at the tiller and the boat was chugging away from the jetty.

'Pipped at the post!' Dave groaned. 'In another couple of minutes he'll be on the mainland and riding away on that bike with our hundred and fifty pounds. Then we'll never see him or the money again.'

His hands tightened on Havoc's reins and he legged the black to a greater effort. Misty must have thought it was a race because she thrust out her neck and galloped full speed after them. Just behind us thudded Patch and Moonlight with Robin behind, shouting excitedly and urging on Dougal whose short legs were twinkling at twice their usual speed.

Dave rode Havoc up the mound above the ferry-jetty. Then, dropping his reins, he cupped his hands to his mouth to shout:

'Ben, you've got a thief aboard. He's stolen all our savings. Don't let him get away!'

We cheered as Ben, understanding the urgency of the message, swung the tiller over, and brought the ferry (plus the now-protesting Eddie) back to the island.

Madly we cantered down to the jetty and, as the ferry tied up, we jumped off our ponies and swarmed round Eddie as he stepped ashore.

'Got you!' Dave said firmly, seizing him by the arms. 'We'll teach you that crime doesn't pay. We're going to frog-march you back to the cottage, and then telephone the police!'

CHAPTER THIRTEEN

TRICKED!

'Telephone the police!' Eddie challenged. 'Yeh, that'd be the best way of proving a fella's innocence. O.K.! So you're not trusting me? Think I'm bluffing, do you?' He stood in front of Dave, raised his arms and said: 'Go on, search me, matie.'

We watched as Dave ran his hands over Eddie in the way we had seen detectives do on the television. Then, as though for good measure, Eddie turned out his pockets and put the contents on a bollard.

'Me own wallet with a couple of quid in it,' Eddie detailed. 'Driving licence. Union card—the lot! Take my name and address if you like. Get your blinkin' police to check up on me as well.'

Babs and I gazed at each other, baffled. So the thief wasn't Eddie after all!

Suddenly Dave jumped into the boat. 'Our money wasn't on you because you've probably hidden it somewhere here.'

Helped by Ben he searched behind the thwarts, in the stern, under the coils of rope, looking anywhere that a thief might have hidden his loot.

Last of all, they examined Eddie's bike and his duffel bag. But there was no sign of the money. Dave scratched his head, nonplussed.

So we had made a mistake! There had been other people about on the island. By pin-pointing our suspicions on 'Honest' Eddie, had we let the real thief get away? These were the doubts that went through our minds.

Meanwhile, old Ben, the ferryman, had been looking from one to the other of us, not knowing what to make of it all.

'You'd have a job getting hold of Garvice, the policeman,' Ben said. 'He's been drafted over with a score of others to keep order at the Pop Festival at Crampton.'

'Too bad,' said Eddie. 'Ah, well! You can give him my name and address. One of his oppos at Borley can come and check our house.' He turned to us. 'And now, if you cowpokes haven't got any objection, I'll be on my way.'

He got back into the boat and old Ben, with a shake of his head, cast off with 'Honest' Eddie in the stern.

'I don't know whether I believe Eddie or not,' Babs said baffled, with her foot in Patch's stirrup. 'What *has* happened to that money?'

On the way back to the cottage, we searched the ground beside the path, poking sticks into rabbit holes, moving boulders, investigating clumps of gorse and heather in case Eddie had hidden the takings somewhere on his way to the ferry. We felt he might have wanted to get rid of the evidence quickly in case he was challenged. Then, later, he might have planned to come back for the loot.

We questioned all the holidaymakers that we met, and Cedric and his mother. None of them had seen Eddie hide anything, and all of them promised to be on the look out and alert us if they saw him come back.

'I suppose we shouldn't have kept all that money in the cottage,' Dave groaned, as at last we unsaddled the ponies to turn them loose. 'Probably we ought to have put it in a bank, but by the time we'd finished giving the rides and gone across to the mainland, all the banks would have been shut.'

'We've been frightful chumps,' sighed Felicity. 'The least we could have done would have been to lock the cottage door.'

'I suppose we've been too trusting,' said Babs.

I was quiet as I lifted off Misty's saddle and rubbed her back to restore the circulation. One beastly follow-up of a theft was that innocent people were often suspected. I tried to put the thought from me. Several holidaymakers in the other cottages were hard up. Then, of course, there were the day visitors and, next to Eddie, perhaps number two suspect was Cedric! We'd had proof of his greed. Might he not have been tempted to grab all the pony-ride takings as well as his ten per cent? Of course, he'd guess that the money was hidden somewhere in the cottage. With an effort I stopped myself from voicing this suspicion. I knew that the others would be thinking on the same lines, but none of us would want to say anything without proof.

With these unhappy thoughts, I unbuckled the throat-lash of Misty's bridle and lifted it over her ears.

As my pony moved away, I noticed that she was walking unevenly with her near-hind. I watched closely. She wasn't actually lame but there was a definite lack of confidence about the way she was putting her foot to the ground.

'Misty!' I ran after her. 'Let me have a look.'

Not wanting to be caught again just then, my pony threw up her head and cantered away. As she crossed the path I heard the unmistakable clatter of a loose shoe on the stones.

'Oh dear!' I sighed. 'That means a visit to the smithy tomorrow, and one lot less of pony-earnings on the beach.'

'Two,' said Dave firmly, turning to Babs and me. 'I was noticing both your ponies this morning, Jackie and Babs. It's over a month since they were shod. Both Patch and Misty will have to have their feet checked. If their shoes are loose, they might catch in something and tear off, damaging the walls of their hooves. You oughtn't to have waited for something to go wrong. You ought to have had them seen to days ago.' Then he added: 'Pony-girls! Scatterbrains! Madcaps! If I didn't chase you two all the time, you could cause chaos.'

Babs and I had to wait next day until low tide

to take Misty and Patch to be shod, so it wasn't until about four o'clock in the afternoon that we left the Sandbay smithy with four bright new shoes on each pony.

We knew that we wouldn't be back at the beach in time to give any more riders that day so, hitching up Misty and Patch in the stable yard of the inn, we let ourselves be tempted to do some shop-window gazing. Licking strawberry ice-cream cornets we gazed at the variety of bits, bridles, saddles and switches in the local leather shop. We were about to move on to the Beachwear Boutique when something in an Estate Agent's window caught our gaze.

A young man was just fixing a display. We pressed nearer to the window, hardly able to believe what we saw. On the board were three photographs of Pony Island—the cottages, a beach scene and the Shadow Pony.

In bold lettering beneath them were the words:

PONY ISLAND FOR SALE

Just on the market. By order of the owner who has decided to remain in Australia. This desirable investment proposition with excellent money-making potential. Specially attractive to holiday-camp operators, caravan site developers and pop-festival organisers. Offers invited prior to Public Auction.

'Cedric's aunt must be typical of the rest of the family!' exclaimed Babs, when we had partly recovered from our astonishment.

106

'Pony Island's an absolutely unique place,' I said. 'There's nowhere like it anywhere else in Britain, and the Chivers family are prepared to ruin it all, just to make a lot of money out of it.'

'There ought to be a law about it,' Babs declared indignantly. 'Isn't there anything anyone can do to stop it, I wonder?' She broke off. 'I know! There used to be a map of the protected areas in that side street off the square.'

'Yes,' I remembered, 'in the offices of the Society for the Preservation of the Rural Beauty of Southern Britain.'

'Come on.' Babs caught at my arm and together we hurried towards the Society's offices, on the door of which was a notice saying: *Knock and enter.*

A dark-haired young woman of about twenty looked up from her typewriter as we went in. Thrilled and surprised, we recognised her as Angela Goodwood, a well-known local show-jumper and leading light of the Riding Club. She was also a prolific journalist. We had often read her reports in the county newspaper of gymkhanas, point-to-points and other horsy events. We'd also heard and seen her interviews with pony and horse personalities on local radio and TV.

'What a stroke of luck!' Babs said impulsively. 'You're just the person we want to see, Miss Goodwood. We've had the shock of our lives ...'

We told her about the display card that had

been put into the Estate Agent's window and were encouraged when Angela Goodwood seemed to be just as shocked as we were.

'How disgraceful!' she exclaimed. 'Pony Island's in the process of being scheduled as a preservation area of outstanding natural beauty. You've certainly done the Society a good turn by drawing our attention to the offer for sale. We'll have to move quickly now. I'm only Secretary of the Society, but luckily our President, Colonel Drummond, is available. In fact, I'm going to see him this evening.'

Then she brought out a note-pad and made notes as she questioned us, explaining to us that publicity could act as a useful rallying call when you had a good cause.

'I'm sure you've got an interesting news story to tell,' she prompted. 'Now, if you'll tell me how you came to be involved with Pony Island . . .'

Babs and I found ourselves explaining how we had found Robin's runaway pony and first become friendly with the Lees; how their house had been burnt down so that they were homeless; how their mother and father had taken a living-in job at a Golf Club, renting Seashell Cottage so that the children had somewhere to live for the summer; how we were helping Dave, Felicity and Robin to earn money for the ponies' winter keep by giving beach rides; and all about the threat from the ton-up boys and the pony takings being stolen.

As fast as the words tumbled from our lips,

Angela Goodwood wrote them down in short-hand.

While we were talking the church clock struck six. Babs and I looked at each other in dismay.

'Goodness!' I gasped. 'The tide will be over the causeway. We'll have to hurry if we're going to get the ponies across to the island tonight.'

Angela was anxious on our behalf and did not want to delay us any further.

'Thanks for your help,' she said briskly. 'I'll be in touch. Don't take any chances over the causeway and, if you can't get across, telephone me at this number.'

CHAPTER FOURTEEN

IN DISGRACE WITH DAVE

'The sea's right over the causeway, but we can still get across if we hurry. Come on, Jackie.'

Before I could deter her, Babs rode Patch straight into the water as it lapped over the cobbles. Misty jibbed, and I had misgivings as I followed my cousin. However, Babs, with the water up to Patch's stifles, was already a quarter of the way across.

'Don't dither, Jackie!' she called over her shoulder. 'It's all right.'

I knew that Babs was being foolhardy but I had to follow because, if I stayed on the mainland side, she might try to turn Patch and come back to me. Then the pony might lose his footing in the swirling water and be swept off the causeway.

Misty was not keen about making the crossing so I had to drive her on with my heels and soon the water was eddying round my feet. Another few yards and the ponies would have to swim for it. Since the current was so strong they might be sucked into a whirlpool and drowned.

Panic gripped me and I had to force myself not to lose my head. Misty seemed to sense that I was afraid. I felt her gather her quarters under her ready to whip round and bolt.

Just as the position seemed hopeless, I saw

Dave running along the shingle of the island beach, dashing to our rescue.

'Don't come any farther,' he shouted. 'Stay where you are and wait for me.'

As I closed my legs to Misty's sides to keep her steady, I saw Babs ahead of me rein up Patch. Then Dave was in the water, wading across the causeway, waist-deep. The sea was up to his chest and, to gain speed, he swam the last three metres, defeating the current with a powerful crawl stroke.

Misty was trembling beneath me. The water was almost to her withers and it took me all my time to make her stand there while Dave grasped Patch's head.

'Hold on, Jackie. I'll be back for you and Misty in a minute,' he called as he led the skewbald forward.

Patch was forced to swim until his feet again touched the solid ground of the causeway. Dave led him to the shallower water. Then Dave turned and came back for Misty and me.

Feeling Dave's grasp on her bridle, my pony dug in her toes and shivered. She was reluctant to leave the firm ground for the swirling water. I had to hit her with my switch before she would yield to Dave's tugs. Nervously, she edged forward until the sea lifted her off her feet. With rapid movements of her legs and helped by Dave's guiding hand at her head, she breasted the current and swam a few metres until her feet again touched the causeway. Then, before I

111

could stop her, she shook her head free of Dave's grip, splashed past him, almost pushing him off the cobbles back into the sea and, picking up her feet, high-stepped through the shallows to the beach.

'Thank you, Dave.' Babs jumped down from Patch to thump him on the back as he bent to squeeze the water from his trouser legs. 'You were wonderful.'

'Yes, a real hero,' I agreed whole-heartedly. 'You saved our ponies' lives.'

Dave's eyes flashed as he turned on us in justifiable exasperation. 'For Pete's sake, spare me the gratitude! You're about the silliest ponygirls I've had the misfortune to meet, and believe me, I've met plenty. We had dozens hanging around our old home.'

Chastened, while Dave's reproaches fell around us, we made a damp and sorry procession as we led the ponies to the cottage.

'You had ample time—three whole hours—to get those ponies shod and get back safely,' Dave said in despair. 'I went to the trouble to telephone the smithy to check that he'd done the job promptly so that you wouldn't miss the tide. Then, what happens? Feckless, without a thought for your ponies' safety or my peace of mind, you dawdle around Sandbay. Then you plunge across the causeway when the tide's far too high, without sizing up the situation. What the dickens did you think you were doing? And where, in heaven's name, did you loaf around for an hour or more?'

'Shall I tell him?' Babs asked, and I realised that—for the first time—she was actually scared of Dave, 'or will you, Jackie?'

'It's a long story——' I began.

'Save it till later,' Dave grunted looking fierce. Then his face screwed up as he unsuccessfully tried to stifle a sneeze. *'Atishoo!'*

As we reached Seashell Cottage we remembered, to our chagrin that yesterday Dave had started a summer cold. His ducking would be sure to make it worse.

He turned his head to sneeze again and, this time, the echo of it rebounded from the cottage walls and, as though in sympathy, Patch—who had swallowed seawater—coughed. Then Misty whinnied. From the Chivers's cottage, Tweetie barked. Meanwhile, Cedric, dazzling in scarlet shirt and blue sailcloth trousers, appeared at the door. Removing his dark glasses, he stared at us in surprise, before bursting into mocking laughter.

'More pony bother!' he called over his shoulder towards the cottage. 'Don't miss this, Ma. It'll make your day. The water-logged wonders ride again!'

'Cedric makes me mad,' Dave grumbled feelingly. 'He seems to think this newspaper report is just a giggle. I think it's terrible. Look at this!'

He pushed a copy of the local newspaper under our startled eyes two days later.

'What do you two think you've been doing?' he went on as we read Angela's article. 'Blabbing all our family business to a journalist!'

'We're dreadfully sorry,' I said consolingly. 'I know it may be shaming for you, but it might do good.'

'A lot of good,' endorsed Babs, scanning the newsprint. 'It says here that the preservation society is opening a fund to save Pony Island and that it's asking the local Council for a grant.'

'And look at this,' I pointed out. 'Colonel Drummond is forming a vigilante patrol to guard the causeway at weekends against the ton-up boys. Then they won't be able to molest the ponies, do any more stealing or damage the Shadow Pony.'

'That's all very well.' Dave still sounded exasperated. 'But why did you have to tell this woman all about our Dad coming out of the Navy, and our house being burned down? How would you like it if all your family affairs were blazoned in the newspapers? What will Mum and Dad think when they hear about it? Pony-girls! Typical!'

He glared at us both in turn as though we were the most hopeless girls he'd ever met. 'You two really are the limit,' he added. 'I'd never have agreed to your coming here in the first place if I'd known you were going to do anything like this.'

An indignant gleam came to Babs' eyes. 'You're nothing but a grouch and a spoil-sport, David Lee!' she exclaimed before I could stop her. 'You don't deserve such a super sister and brother as Felicity and Robin. If you don't watch it, you'll grow up to be the kind of cross-patch that everyone will hate and you won't have any friends at all. I wish we'd never met you.'

'That goes for me, too!' Dave exclaimed, and broke off to stifle a sneeze. 'Now, listen, you pair will do me a favour by getting off this island and taking your ponies with you! Understand?'

As he strode out of the cottage, I ran after him, plucking at his pullover.

'Babs didn't mean it,' I told him. 'You saved our ponies' lives, Dave. We both think the world of you all, especially you, Dave. Give us another chance. Let us stay a few more days,' I begged, 'Just over the weekend, at least.'

'Until Monday, then.' Dave shook off my grasp. 'But watch your step, both of you! Another blunder and you're barred from the island for ever.'

'It sounds as though we're not going to have a

wasted day, after all,' Angela Goodwood declared to the waiting television camera crew as we heard the roar of approaching motor-cycles that Saturday afternoon. 'Are you ready to film, boys? I can dub on the commentary afterwards.'

The cameras panned from the approaching leather-boys to the side of the Ferry Inn where, out of sight for the moment, Colonel Drummond waited with two of his friends. As the motor-cycles roared nearer, the three men stepped forward and placed hurdles—borrowed from the local Riding Club—across the road to bar the approach to the causeway.

'That's it, lads,' Colonel Drummond said to the leather-boys, standing firmly in front of the barricades. 'No entry.'

'So you think that you're going to stop us, do you, Grandad? Put the mockers on our day out?' challenged the leader of the ton-up boys, revving his bike and menacing the Colonel. 'You and these other two old geezers? Pop Eye and Walrus Whiskers? You'll be lucky!'

Colonel Drummond, Commodore Wintropp and Wing-Commander Greville-Paget stood firm, and Angela Goodwood signalled to the camera team to move in closer to film the eye-ball confrontation.

'So we're all having our pictures taken?' One of the leather-boys waved to the camera. 'See you on the box tonight, Ma!'

'Cut the cackle, Freddie,' said one of the others. 'Let's have some action.'

'Where's Eddie?' demanded Babs. 'Too scared to come?'

'Don't be rough with the Army, Navy and Air Force,' the leader said cheekily ignoring Babs 'Let's just give them a nice bathe in the drink. That'll wash the cobwebs off them.'

Propping up their machines, the ton-up boys advanced on Colonel Drummond and his friends. Dave was already moving forward with clenched fists to help to defend Pony Island, and Babs, Felicity, Robin and I were behind him, feeling scared. We knew that Colonel Drummond had planned a surprise strategy, but we felt anxious that he seemed to be delaying putting it into action. It wasn't until the motor-cycle bullies were six metres from him that he turned to the Ferry Inn and shouted an order.

'Reinforcements at the double, please!'

From the Inn surged the fifteen members of the Rugby Club's team. In a brawny body they bore down on the leather-boys.

'Who said something about a dip in the briny?' shouted the scrum-half, making for the leader, while a forward picked up one of the machines as though he was about to fling it into the sea.

Meanwhile the camera-team dodged around to get the most telling action-scenes.

'Terrific!' Dave said to me, his eyes agleam with excitement. 'I'm only sorry that Eddie isn't here to be taught a lesson. The fact that he's stayed away shows he's got our money somewhere, I should think.'

As they had intended, the Rugby players won a complete victory within two minutes, without having to strike a single blow. Like most bullies, the leather-boys were cowards at heart. They cringed, backed, yelped, and scrambled on their bikes and retreated in an untidy rabble back up the hill.

'Thank you, men,' Colonel Drummond said to the Rugby Fifteen. 'Mission accomplished.'

'Hurrah!' cheered Robin. 'Victory without a shot being fired.'

Meanwhile holidaymakers, who had been

alerted by the noise, flocked round Angela to sign a petition to the County Council requesting them to make an order for the preservation of Pony Island. Dave, still wretched from his cold, was relieved that the vigilantes were there to help fend off the vandals.

'I was looking forward to tackling Eddie,' he told us later. I wanted to shake the truth out of him, but he didn't dare to come, the rat! Pity! So, we're no nearer finding out what he did with our takings. I wonder whether we'll ever see him —or our money—again?'

CHAPTER FIFTEEN

SURPRISE! SURPRISE!

The following day was Sunday.

'Our last day on the island,' I sighed, lengthening Misty's stirrups after giving a ride to a very young rider. 'Dave hasn't said anything, so I suppose he's not going to let us stay.'

'I can't bear to think of it——' began Babs.

'Do you do longer rides?' interrupted a ten-year-old girl who was standing by, clutching her money. 'My sister and I wanted to ride up to the Shadow Pony. We don't mind paying thirty-pence each for a really long ride.'

'Right,' I said briskly, trying to keep up my spirits. 'Get on the ponies.'

We ran alongside as the two girls bounced up and down on Misty and Patch, and ten minutes later paused for a breather by the shadow rocks.

We had a clear view of the Sound between Pony Island and the mainland. Suddenly I caught sight of a youth between the two ferry-jetties where the water was deep at every state of the tide.

'Why should anyone skin-dive there?' puzzled Babs, 'unless he was trying to recover something valuable?'

'Yes, such as over a hundred and fifty pounds of pony-takings in silver and notes in a plastic bag,' I added, following her train of thought, 'which he might have slipped over the stern of the ferry boat! Gosh! It could be Eddie. We must tell Dave.'

Explaining to the two riders, and promising them another ride later, Babs and I mounted Misty and Patch and galloped back to alert Dave that Eddie had returned to the scene of his crime.

With Robin and Dougal bringing up the rear we raced across the island to the ferry-jetty.

'Look!' Felicity pointed as she reined up. 'He's surfacing now. It could be Eddie!'

We watched the skin-diver's rubber-helmeted head break the ripples. He seemed to adjust his goggles. Then, with a kick of his frog-flippers, he dived again, to appear a few moments later, holding something.

'It's the plastic bag with the money!' Robin reported excitedly. 'See! It's tied up with Felicity's old ribbon.'

'You're right, Babs,' gasped Dave. 'He's swimming ashore now. "Honest" Eddie my foot! Come on!'

'He led our headlong gallop down the slope. It was almost high-tide and the causeway was under almost two metres of water as Dave made for the pebbly beach.

'Leave this to me,' he called over his shoulder. 'I'm going to swim Havoc across.'

He drove Havoc forward. Then the black

gelding, feeling the swirl of the tide under him, panicked. He reared, came over backwards and ended threshing in the water while Dave was thrown off.

To our horror, Dave suddenly seemed motionless. He was floating in the current. His head must have struck a rock when he was thrown. He was stunned, unable to help himself, and the skirl of the water was pulling him away.

Havoc, too, was in peril. Having lost his footing, he'd been carried into the deeper water.

The fact that Dave's and Havoc's lives were in jeopardy, put all thoughts of Eddie and the money right out of our minds.

We had only one purpose now—to save Dave and Havoc.

Leaving our ponies on the shingle, Felicity, Robin, Babs and I waded into the waves. Still motionless and face downwards, Dave was floating on the current into a backwater between the rocks. Once there, we'd never be able to reach him.

Babs and I fought our way through the swirling water. At last we reached him. Desperately Babs grabbed at one ankle while I held the other. Waist-deep, we floundered backwards, tugging Dave towards the shore.

He moaned and spluttered as we turned him over on the pebbles and pumped his arms to make him gulp in air. He sneezed and we knew that he had come round. We raced back into the waves to help Felicity and Robin who, by now, had Havoc by the bridle and were pulling him into shallower water.

I grabbed one of Havoc's stirrups and Babs caught his mane. Between us all, we dragged him from the current. Then, his feet were on solid ground, and—with a snort and heave—we lumbered out of the water and walked unsteadily up the shingle.

Coughing and choking, Dave struggled to his feet. There was anger and defeat in his face as he gazed across the Sound.

On the other side, we could see Eddie struggling through the mud to the shore. As we watched, he turned to make a gesture of contempt in our direction.

Defiantly he held up the plastic bag with the pony-takings as though to taunt us.

Half-drowned and marooned by the tide on Pony Island, we were unable to stop him.

'He's outwitted us!' groaned Babs. 'What do we do now?'

'If only old Ben were here with his motor-boat!' Felicity sighed.

'He is!' I exclaimed. 'Look!'

We saw the ferry chugging against the current, Ben at the wheel, and two men with rods in the stern. They were returning from a fishing trip.

Hurriedly tying up our ponies, we dashed to the jetty and piled in the ferry as it drew alongside.

'Quick, Ben!' Dave explained to the ferryman, gesticulating towards Eddie who was still floundering, frog-flippered, through the mud. 'We need your help.'

Four minutes later, I felt like cheering when we all formed a semi-circle on the mainland beach—a welcome-party for Eddie as he staggered ashore, mud still dragging at his flippers. Outnumbered, he didn't offer much resistance when Dave snatched the plastic bag from him.

'Our hard-earned takings!' Dave whooped in triumph. 'Thanks, my lad. A right villain you've turned out to be—almost as bad as your cousin Cedric.'

'Cousin!' glared Eddie. 'How do you know Ced's my cousin?'

'Just a guess,' said Dave. 'There is a likeness

though. You've both got the same mean, greedy eyes.'

'And the same sneaky, nasty natures,' added Babs.

'So that's that!' said old Ben, the ferryman. 'And seeing as how I brought young Cedric and his Ma over from the island—bag and baggage— no more than a couple of hours ago, I reckon that gets the whole of the Chivers family out of your hair.'

'Chivers!' echoed Felicity. 'You mean Gumby. They're impostors as well as thieves.'

'Left the island!' Eddie turned to Ben in amazement. 'Do you mean to say Aunty Zena and Ced have made a getaway? The double-crossers! So they've tricked me. They said that they'd take me with them and give me a share of the money——'

'Ah, yes,' Dave deduced. 'You mean the money they got by swindling people who wanted to buy the holiday cottages. That must have been why your Aunty Zena wanted so many prints of the photos of the cottages. I suppose she advertised them as "Bargain Holiday Cottages For Sale. Send for photo, but hurry! One hundred pounds deposit secures".'

'Why, I bet they were "selling" the same cottages several times over, getting scores of deposits—and then scarpering,' Babs concluded. 'The wretches!'

'Crikey!' Eddie groaned. 'You lot have found out everything. Been clever, ain't you? Well, I'm

125

not taking the blame for Ced's and Aunty's swindle. I'll tell all. Then I might get off lightly over helping myself to your pony-money.'

'Talk—and talk fast,' Robin directed, assuming the role of a TV 'tec.

'They planned this months ago,' Eddie told us. 'They're no relation to the Chiverses. The real Chiverses are in Australia. Ced and his Ma answered an advert to caretake these cottages while the Chiverses were away.'

'Then they hatched this plot,' I added.

'Yes, and if you're not nippy they'll get away with it,' Eddie warned. 'They'll be at the airport now, waiting to catch a 'plane to sunny Spain, and with thousands of pounds in a false compartment in their suitcases. You'll have to hurry.'

'I'll 'phone the police. They'll radio the airport to hold the Gumbys.' Already dashing up the Beach Dave called back over his shoulder: 'Stand guard over Eddie until the law comes.'

Babs had never cooked sausage and mash—Dave's favourite meal—to look so delicious as it did that evening for our celebration supper. We ware just about to start eating when a holiday-maker who had already moved into the Gumbys' cottage appeared at the door.

'Trunk call for you, David,' she said. 'It's your Dad on the line.'

Dave tore himself away from his sausage and mash and Babs popped his plate into the oven to keep warm. We'd all finished ours before Dave

126

came back, and Felicity and Robin looked eagerly towards him to hear what he had to report.

'What's the news?' asked Robin.

'*Atish-oo!* Ha-ha!'

Dave had to keep us in suspense as his sneeze changed into a carefree laugh, and I realised I had never seen him look so happy and relaxed. Despite his shocking cold all his troubles seemed to have vanished.

'Terrific news!' he declared, while I got his sausage and mash from the oven. 'Mum and Dad are thrilled. They read about the Battle of the Causeway in the newspapers. Then Colonel Drummond telephoned Dad. He said that the preservation society has bought Pony Island and the committee want Mum and Dad to live here permanently as wardens. They're planning to knock two cottages into one for us.'

'So we'll all have a home together,' said Felicity, hugging Dave, 'and we'll be able to keep the ponies.'

'And Jackie and Babs will be able to stay with us here on Pony Island whenever they like,' added Robin. 'Won't they, Dave?'

'Of course,' Dave said warmly. 'They're two pony-girls in a million.'

That night, before Babs and I climbed into bed, we gazed out of the bedroom window at the ponies dozing in the moonlight while the Shadow Pony galloped over the silvered turf.

How wonderful it was to think that the island

would be unspoiled, and that Felicity, Robin, Dave and their parents and ponies would have a permanent home in this magical place.

'Sleep well, ponies,' I murmured. 'There are lots of super days ahead of you . . . and for all of us.'

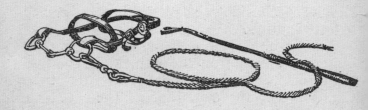